The boy from the
UFO returns

The boy from the
UFO returns

(Original title: Barney in Space)

by MARGARET GOFF CLARK

illustrated by TED LEWIN

SCHOLASTIC BOOK SERVICES

NEW YORK · TORONTO · LONDON · AUCKLAND · SYDNEY · TOKYO

ACKNOWLEDGMENTS

The author wishes to thank: William Baran, Chairman, Science Department, Niagara Wheatfield Central School, for checking the manuscript; and the workshop of the Association of Professional Women Writers.

0-590-32509-4

12 11 10 9 8 7 6 5 4 3 2 1   2   3 4 5 6/8

Printed in the U. S. A.   11

For Dody and Toby,

friends for all seasons

CONTENTS

Another Book by Margaret Goff Clark,
published by Scholastic

The Boy from the UFO
(Original title: Barney and the UFO)

The boy from the
UFO returns

No Footprints

"Let's go!" cried Barney.

With hair flying, he ran down the snowy driveway toward the woodshed to get logs for the fireplace. His Irish terrier, Finn McCool, bounded beside him, his furry front legs as straight as sticks.

It was 2:00 P.M., the day after Christmas. Ever since lunch Barney Crandall had been helping his little brother, Scott, operate his new electronic toys.

The air, crisp after last night's snowfall, refreshed him like a cold shower.

How easy it was to run today! His body was light as a balloon. His feet scarcely touched the ground.

He had never before been able to run like this. Was it because his legs were stronger after all the cross-country skiing he had done this winter? Or because he was taller? Since coming to live with the Crandalls seven months ago, he had put on a few inches.

But, no, something more than his new strength and

height was propelling him. Abruptly his joy of a moment ago changed to alarm.

His feet did not seem to reach the ground. There was nothing solid under them. Strangest of all, he no longer heard the crunch of snow as he ran.

Finn had stopped dashing around and was staring at him with his head cocked on one side and a puzzled expression in his round eyes.

Still running, Barney glanced back. Behind him, the fresh snow was smooth and unbroken. He was leaving no footprints!

A stab of terror hit like a knife in his heart. What had happened to him? People always left footprints in the snow.

When he tried to stand still, his fear grew, for his legs kept on pumping, running in air.

Barney reached the woodshed and passed it. Off to his right rose the white mound that was the foundation of Grandfather Crandall's old barn, all that was left of the building. In front of him stretched the wide, snow-covered meadow, sloping gradually up the side of Mount Casper, one of the tallest peaks in the foothills of the Catskill Mountains. No matter how he tried to stop, he couldn't. Barney was being drawn toward the mountain.

He was dimly aware of the sound of an upstairs window being opened in the house behind him.

His mother's call reached him. "Barney! Where are you going?"

At the sound of her voice, Barney felt himself dropping, sinking inches deep into the snow. He staggered, trying to keep his balance, then turned around to face the house.

"I don't know!" he cried. "Something happened. I don't know what. Something weird!"

"Well, come in, come in! Tell me about it!" His mother pushed the window shut.

His heart racing with excitement, Barney started back. The snow was deep and walking was hard work. On the way out he had skimmed over this same route like a low-flying bird. Now with each step he had to pull his foot out of a well of snow. Soon he was puffing. But he welcomed the struggle, because he was again in control of his own body.

He passed the woodshed without a pause, forgetting why he had come outside.

What had made him float? And why had he stopped when his mother called? He actually had been flying in the air, not high, but he had been above the ground. Had he had a dream from which his mother's voice awakened him? Could a person sleep and dream while running in the snow?

No, it was not a dream, he told himself firmly. Just now, walking back, he had come through unbroken snow. There had been no footprints except for Finn's.

There had to be a reasonable answer. It wasn't magic. He had been lifted and pulled by some powerful force. He had been as helpless as a carpet tack drawn by a magnet. The force that had raised him above the snow was real, even though he didn't quite understand it.

This wasn't the first time something unusual had happened to him. Last June, soon after he and Scott had come here from the orphanage to live with the Crandalls, he had met someone who had the power to do strange things like this. But that person—or creature—a boy named Tibbo, was far from here by now, on the way to the planet Ornam where he lived.

Barney had a vivid memory of the night when he had first seen the UFO, the spaceship Tibbo piloted. Then he had still been Barney Galloway, orphan. He had been afraid to tell the Crandalls about the UFO for fear they'd change their minds about adopting him and his four-year-old brother.

He shuddered, and not from the cold. His wide, pleasant mouth set in a firm line. The space boy was his friend, but he meant trouble. Tibbo mustn't come again! Not now, when everything was working out so great for him and Scott.

2 Ø

No One Believes

Barney kicked off his snow boots in the hall, rushed through the kitchen, and, with Finn at his heels, took the steps to the second floor two at a time.

His mother was waiting for him at the top of the stairs.

"Mom!" he burst out. "Something wild happened!" He clenched his fists and his breath came in short gasps. "Something unreal!"

"Take it easy!" she urged. "It can't be that bad."

"It is! You don't know!"

Barney paced back and forth in the hall, so upset he was ready to explode. Finn followed him, whining, as if worried by his master's strange actions.

His mother flung out her arms with one of the quick gestures that made her seem so young, so full of life. "*What* happened?"

"I ran and I didn't touch the ground!"

"Of course you were on the ground." It was his

15

mother's no-nonsense tone of voice. "Come on." She led him into the sewing room and pulled him down beside her on the couch. "I was sitting right there, working on my dress for the New Year's party." She pointed to the machine in front of the south window where a piece of silky gold material lay like a strip of sunshine. "I looked out and saw you running. I wondered how you could run that fast in the snow. But you were on the ground."

"No, I wasn't! I didn't make footprints!"

"That's impossible." She shook her head vigorously, making her straight dark hair swirl around her head. When he gazed back at her steadily, she appeared bewildered, as if she were trying to get hold of a memory. Slowly she asked, "Didn't you have a strange experience last summer?"

"Yes!" said Barney eagerly. "Remember when I saw the UFO—the spaceship—behind the house? It was like a silver ball with a ring around it. And then the boy who was in the UFO talked to me. I couldn't see him, but I could hear his voice, something like radio . . ."

He halted because his mother didn't seem to understand. She was staring at him almost as if he had lost his mind.

"Barney, Barney, what are you talking about?" She looked distressed enough to cry. "I don't remember

16

anything like *that*. And I've never known you to make up stories.''

Somehow he had to make her believe. He tried again. "No, Mom. It isn't a story. It's true. I think that boy from the UFO is back again. He must be the one who made me float.''

She stood up briskly. "It's all right to have an imagination, but you have to keep in mind what is made up and what is true.''

"I do know what's true," he began miserably. He had lost the fear that had seized him when he realized he was floating above the ground. Now the most important thing was to convince his mother it had really happened.

"Come on.'' She picked up a jacket from a chair and moved toward the hall. "Let's go out in back and look at the snow where you walked.''

Barney hurried after her, encouraged. She would see the one set of footprints heading back to the house and then she'd believe him.

They were on the way to the back door, still followed by Finn, when Scott zoomed into the kitchen, holding high the space rocket Barney had given him for Christmas. A sturdy little fellow, square shouldered like his brother, he skidded to a halt in front of Barney.

"The fire's almost out. You said you were going to get some more wood.''

"I forgot. I'll bring some in a minute. You keep Finn, will you?"

"Okay." Scott sped off, making a rocket-engine noise.

Barney and his mother went out the back door and started down the driveway, making sure not to step in the footprints already in the snow.

"There are two sets," his mother said. "I can see them plainly."

"Sure," he agreed. "Here I hadn't started to float, not till just before I came to the woodshed."

Finn's feet had trotted across some of the tracks but, to Barney's relief, just beyond the woodshed the single line of prints marched plainly back toward the house.

His mother studied them in silence. "You're right, Son. I don't know how you did it, but the footprints go only one way." She gazed at him seriously. "Is this some kind of trick?"

Barney felt a heaviness in his chest. She didn't believe him, even with the evidence right in front of her. "No, it isn't a trick," he said.

"Go call Dad," she said. "He's in the cellar, working on those shelves for the storeroom."

When Barney charged down the basement steps, his father was sawing a plank. He wouldn't mind being interrupted; Barney knew that. This strong, friendly man who had adopted him and Scott was always ready to help or listen.

Now he put aside his work and pulled on his coat while Barney explained about his strange experience and reminded him of the boy from outer space who had come last summer.

"You remember Tibbo. He wanted me to go back to his planet. Ornam, it's called," said Barney, "and the people on it are called Garks."

"You've lost me." Mr. Crandall laughed. "What TV show was that on?"

"It wasn't on TV," Barney said impatiently. What was the matter with his parents that they couldn't remember? "You saw the UFO yourself. It came down in the meadow."

His father zipped up his jacket, his eyes on Barney's flushed face. "What's this all about? You've always been as sensible as—as I am. And honest, absolutely honest."

"You couldn't forget!" cried Barney. But his father's puzzled expression made it plain he had forgotten. Barney clung to hope. "Wait till you see the footprints."

But his father had a quick answer to the single line of footprints. "That's an old trick," he said gruffly. "I used to do it myself. You turned around out there where the snow's all chewed up." He pointed to the place

19

where Barney had sunk into the snow when his mother called. "Then you walked back, putting your feet into the same prints you made on the way out." He put his arm around Barney's shoulders. "Right, Son?"

Barney pulled away, his eyes burning. Through stiff lips he managed to say, "I wouldn't play tricks on you and Mom."

He stalked angrily toward the woodshed for the logs he had forgotten earlier.

His parents had often told him, "Talk things over with us."

Great! What good did it do to talk when they didn't believe him and they couldn't even remember something that happened only a few months ago?

Their forgetting Tibbo and the UFO was weird. It was almost as strange as his running above the snow.

3 Ø

Someone Remembers

Barney was on the way out of the woodshed with the logs when the Crandalls caught up with him.

His mother put a hand on his shoulder. "We know you wouldn't play a trick to be mean."

His father closed the door of the shed for him. "Right! But when you do pull off a trick, afterward you say April Fool! Or whatever."

They hadn't believed in the UFO last summer, either, Barney recalled. Not until they saw it.

He managed a smile. "It wasn't a trick, but don't worry about it," he said, trying not to show how much he was hurt by their disbelief. "I think I'll ski over and talk to Dick." Dick Williams, his best friend and junior-high classmate, lived less than half a mile away, on the edge of Pineville, the nearest town. Everyone agreed Dick was a brain. If anyone could figure out why Barney had floated, Dick could do it.

"Fine," said his father.

When Barney went into the family room carrying the wood, Scott, with the rocket ship on the coffee table beside him, was stretched out on the davenport, half asleep. He scarcely stirred when his brother rekindled the fire. Finn, on the hearth rug, opened his eyes sleepily, then closed them. Christmas had worn both of them out, Barney thought.

Minutes later Barney was on his way to Dick's, the hood of his blue jacket covering his shock of hair.

The snow was ideal for skiing. Following beside the road, he tried to keep in mind all that his father had taught him about cross-country skiing. Relax. Keep a rhythmic stride and don't depend too much on your poles.

But, in a hurry to talk with Dick, he pushed himself harder than usual and soon he was perspiring.

The road was extra busy today, and many of the cars had loaded ski racks. Barney was glad he lived in the country where all he had to do was go out the door and take off. He had never skied until this winter, but with the first good snowfall his father had taken him out. Since then he had rarely missed a day's practice.

Dick was in his room, putting dabs of various things onto a slide and looking at them through his new microscope. He was crazy about any kind of science.

"Look here, Barney," he said. "This is sour milk."

He was bending over his microscope with his straight brown hair falling over his forehead. "What d'you think of that?"

Barney obediently peered through the eyepiece and then moved away so Dick could have another look. The squiggles on the slide meant little to him. He didn't see why his friend got such a charge out of science. Now motors, anything mechanical, that was his idea of fun.

"That's great," he said, "but I wanted to talk to you about something."

Absentmindedly Dick took his eye away from the microscope and straightened his long, lean body. "What's up, pal?"

"Uh—something funny happened to me this morning. I was going after some wood—"

"Yeah?" Dick still had a faraway look.

"I was running and I felt great. But then it felt too easy. Y'know, it's usually hard to run in snow. And next thing I knew I was floating."

Dick's eyes snapped to attention. "You were *what?*"

"Floating," said Barney firmly, as if daring Dick to disagree. "I wasn't touching the ground. And something pulled me toward Mount Casper. I tried to stop and I couldn't."

Dick's eyebrows went up like two brown question marks and he gave Barney a wise look. "Christmas

23

must've been real exciting at your house.''

"Come off it, Dick. I'm not kidding. Remember when the spaceship came down and—''

"What spaceship? What are you talking about?''

"Last June. Stop clowning around. *You* remember. I know you do. You were with me and you saw it. You never were able to talk with my space friend, Tibbo, so I had to tell you everything he said.''

But half an hour later Barney gave up. No matter how he tried to make him recall, Dick had no more memory of the spaceship that had landed in the meadow last June than his parents had.

Skiing home in the gathering dusk, Barney felt as if he were living a nightmare. Cars sped past in the December darkness. But Barney, trying to make sense out of his unusual problem, paid no attention to the beams that flashed across him like strobe lights in a disco.

In the weeks since last June, he and Dick had often talked about the boy from Ornam. Lately, busy with school and skiing, the subject hadn't come up. But that still didn't explain why his friend had forgotten anything as important and exciting as the visitor from another planet.

He found his mother in the kitchen with the radio going, playing dance music. All the while she worked, putting out a platter of sliced turkey, lettuce, and to-

24

matoes for sandwiches, she seemed to be keeping time with the music.

Talk about floating! thought Barney. Her feet scarcely touched the floor when she walked or danced.

She came toward him and, with one of her swift motions, thrust a bite of turkey into his mouth. He grinned, and gulped it down before he tried to talk.

"Mom," he said, "this afternoon when I told about how I ran without touching the ground—you said something about—well, anyway—something strange that had happened to me last summer."

She paused with her hand on the refrigerator door. "I did say that, didn't I? I wonder what I meant. I don't remember anything about it now."

She came over to him and studied his serious face. "Are you still thinking about floating?"

He nodded.

With one finger she smoothed the worried pucker between his eyes. "Sometimes a person feels dizzy—maybe has a floating feeling—when he eats something that doesn't agree with him. And yesterday we did have a big dinner and lots of candy and everything."

Barney shook his head, unable to cast off his unhappiness. "I feel all right. I actually did float, you know."

She sighed and went to the stove to turn off the heat under the whistling teakettle.

Barney wandered to the door of the family room, which opened directly off the kitchen. From the doorway he could see the back of the davenport and the fireplace beyond it. As he glanced in, Scott stood up on the cushions and looked sleepily over the back of the sofa at his brother.

Strolling in, Barney ruffled the little boy's already tousled hair. "Come upstairs and I'll help you get sharpened up for supper."

Scott giggled and seized his brother around the neck in a strangle hold.

"Besides," said Barney as they climbed the stairs, "Kara's coming over tonight with her dad and mom."

"That's good." Scott liked Kara MacDougall, a girl about a year younger than Barney who lived a short distance up the road. "For supper?"

"No. Afterward."

They were in Scott's room, and the little boy was sitting on the floor, pulling on a clean sock, when he paused and looked up at Barney.

"I heard you and Mom talking about something in the kitchen. Something about floating. You mean floating like in the water?"

Barney explained. "I felt as if I could fly and when I looked back at the snow there weren't any footprints behind me."

26

Scott put on his other sock, then remarked, "Sounds like Tibbo's back."

"Did you say *Tibbo?*" Excitedly Barney dropped to his knees beside his brother.

Scott nodded. "That boy in the UFO."

Full of happy emotion, Barney scooped him up and hugged him. "You remember!"

For a moment Scott rested his head against Barney's shoulder. Then he pulled free. "Sure."

Barney rubbed his hand across his eyes. His relief was so great he felt close to tears. If his brother remembered, then it was okay. That meant he wasn't crazy.

Scott dived under his bed to retrieve a shoe. When he came out he said solemnly, "I don't want Tibbo to come again."

"I don't either," agreed Barney.

"Don't let him take you away, will you?"

Barney promised. "Never."

4 Ø

Tibbo Returns

That night when the MacDougalls came to the house, Kara was wearing jeans and a new red shirt. Her wavy brown hair was freshly washed and her friendly dark eyes shone.

Scott immediately attached himself to her.

As if he thinks she came to see him, thought Barney.

"Do you think Kara's pretty?" asked Scott.

Barney turned almost as red as Kara's shirt. "Sure."

Kara looked embarrassed and pulled her upper lip down to cover the braces on her teeth. Barney wanted to tell her, "You look okay with braces. Besides, you aren't going to wear them forever." But that would probably make her feel worse. It was better to pretend they were invisible.

Scott pulled her over to the tree to show his presents.

"Want to play my racing car game?" he asked.

Kara glanced at Barney. "I guess so."

But just then Barney's mother sat down at the piano

and began to play *Deck the Halls*, and his father joined in on the new trumpet she had given him for Christmas. Mr. MacDougall's baritone picked up the song and soon everyone was singing. Scott forgot about the game.

Later Mr. Crandall turned on the stereo for dancing. Barney took Kara for a partner. At first he was nervous; then, caught up in the music, he relaxed and enjoyed it.

Finn McCool sat close to the davenport, his eyes alert with interest, but he stayed out of the way of the dancers.

The adults had gone to the living room for bridge, and Barney, Kara, and Scott were playing the car racing game when the little boy suddenly asked, "Barney, did you tell Kara you floated?"

"Floated?" she asked. It was her turn to play and she had been skillfully using the electric control to steer her car. At Scott's remark, though, she was startled and the car jumped the track.

Scott scrambled after it and returned it to her.

"He—floated—in—the—air," he said, emphasizing each word.

Kara sat still, just holding the car and the control in her hands. She looked at Barney with a question in her eyes.

He hesitated; then decided he might as well explain, since Scott had brought up the subject.

When he had finished telling about the way he had

run without touching the snow, Kara asked, "Is Tibbo back again?"

Barney grinned. "You remember, too!" He took the little car from her. "Let's not play this game any more now." He went to the fireplace, poked at the charred logs, and added a fresh one.

Kara sat cross-legged on the rug in front of the davenport and watched him.

"I haven't heard anything from Tibbo," Barney said, "but I thought of him right away, too. Dad and Mom don't remember anything about him."

"They don't!" Kara's eyes widened in amazement. "How could they forget?"

Barney shrugged. "They did."

Kara said with assurance, "I'll always remember that night when Tibbo came after you. I was home with a cold so I didn't see the UFO, but you told me all about it. You said it looked so beautiful."

"Yeah, it did," agreed Barney.

"You never saw Tibbo, did you?"

"Not up close. I heard his voice. He talks the same as we do. Says he learned English listening to TV and radio on the way here from Ornam. I only saw him once, like a shadow in the spaceship."

"I wonder where he is now?" Kara gazed into the fire as if she might see the space boy rising from the flames.

30

"On the way back home to Ornam, I guess. When he left here six months ago he said it would take about five years to get there, even traveling at the speed of light."

Kara drew her knees up to her chin. "I'd hate to stay in a spaceship that long. I get tired of riding in the car when we go to Albany, and that only takes two hours." She gave Barney a penetrating glance. "Maybe Tibbo turned around and came back."

Barney sat down on the raised step in front of the fireplace. "I've been thinking the same thing." He sighed and leaned back against the warm stone. "I like Tibbo, but I wish he'd stay away."

Kara looked surprised. "Why? I'd think it was exciting to talk with someone from another planet."

"It was exciting, all right. When he was around, I never knew what was going to happen next. It messed up my life. Like now. Mom and Dad haven't said much yet, but I can tell they're wondering what's wrong with me. There's no way they're going to believe I'm in touch with someone from outer space."

"Well, I do," said Kara staunchly.

While Kara and Barney talked, Scott had been nearby, looking at one and then another of his new toys. Apparently he had been listening to the conversation, for now he came over and leaned against his brother's knee. "I believe you, too," he said.

Barney kept his eyes on the rug. It was great not to be alone with his problem. But all he could say was, "Thanks, both of you."

The next morning Barney and his father set out on snowshoes to cut down a tree and bring back the wood for the fireplace. They crossed the meadow behind the house, bound for the woodland a short distance up the slope of Mount Casper. They had left Finn home because the snow was too deep for him.

"We still have enough in the shed to last a long while," said Mr. Crandall, "but we have to let fresh wood season, especially if it's green."

"Green wood?" questioned Barney.

"That's what we call wood from a live tree." He laughed. "You city slickers have a lot to learn."

Barney overlapped his snowshoes and almost fell. "I could learn a lot more about walking with these things."

"Want me to pull the toboggan?"

"No. I'll get it all together if I don't break my neck first."

Two hours later they were on the way out of the woodland, both pulling the loaded toboggan. Barney felt tired but contented. It had been fun to look for the best tree to cut.

"We want one that'll burn well and give plenty of heat. Maple's fine," his father had said. "So are birch and beech. But we have to find one we can fell without damaging other good small trees.''

Finally, they chose a maple Barney located.

His father had cut it down with the chain saw, notching the trunk so accurately that the tree dropped exactly where he wanted it.

Barney walked across the snowy ground, managing his snowshoes better than on the way up. He was thinking of dinner and the apple pie he had seen cooling on the kitchen shelf when suddenly his skin began to tingle. A moment later he heard a familiar voice.

''Hi, Barney! Guess who this is?''

''Tibbo!'' exclaimed Barney. ''Where are you?''

His father turned to look at him and asked, ''What did you say?''

Tibbo's sassy voice sounded in Barney's ears. ''Sounds like another station cutting in. He can't hear me talking, you know. Keep still. Think your answers. I'm tuned in to your brain. I even know you're not too pleased to hear from me again.''

Barney managed not to answer out loud. ''I'm gladder than I thought I'd be. Maybe you can tell me why I was floating in the air yesterday.''

''I sure can. You're in danger, Earth friend.''

Barney was concentrating on Tibbo's voice when his father broke in.

''Barney, can't you hear me?''

Before he had time to answer his father, Tibbo interrupted. "If you tell him you're talking to me, I'm leaving. I didn't come here to listen to him ask a lot of questions."

In his indignation Barney forgot to think his answer. "What d'you expect me to do?"

"Watch it!" warned Tibbo.

"Barney, what *are* you talking about?" demanded his father. "Are you all right?"

"Oh, sure, Dad," he answered. "I—I was just talking to myself."

This seemed to anger Tibbo. "Who are you talking to, him or me, or yourself?"

"What can I do?" demanded Barney, remembering to think his answer. "You don't want me to tell Dad you're here."

"I know what *I* can do." Tibbo was his usual independent self. "I can leave."

"Oh, please—" Barney began out loud. Then he stopped. His skin was no longer tingling. That meant his space friend had gone.

5 Ø

An Enemy from Space

Barney and his father stacked the freshly cut wood in the shed behind the house.

All the time he was working, Barney's mind was on the boy from Ornam. "You're in danger, Earth friend," Tibbo had warned. What danger? wondered Barney. Did it have something to do with his floating?

He still felt no tingle on his skin. Probably Tibbo was waiting for him to be alone, so he could talk without interruption. Barney felt desperate. He hadn't wanted Tibbo to return, but now the situation had changed. Tibbo was the only one who could tell him what was going on. He *had* to come back.

After lunch Barney went directly to his room with a book. He closed the door, hoping Scott and everyone else would stay out. Although he waited for more than an hour, Tibbo didn't come.

That evening he was in the family room with his parents and Scott. All of them were watching an exciting hockey game on TV when Barney felt the prickling of his skin that meant Tibbo was zeroing in on him.

Barney groaned inwardly. He longed to see the game, but even more he wanted to know—he was frantic to learn—about his own danger.

Slowly he got to his feet and started out of the room. Finn trotted after him, but when Barney said "Stay!" the dog obediently returned to the rug by the fire.

"Hurry back!" called his father, smiling at him.

"Let me know what happens," answered Barney.

He took the steps two at a time, strode into his room, and closed the door behind him.

"Well!" said Tibbo's voice. "It's about time you arrived. Here I am traveling millions of miles to help you, and can you and I get a word alone? No."

"I was here in my room for an hour right after lunch, waiting."

"Yeah? Sorry I missed you." Tibbo didn't sound sorry. "Someone else was using the ship's only Earth scanner," he explained, "so I couldn't locate you until now."

Barney sat down on the edge of the bed. "You said I'm in danger. What do you mean?"

"Rokell is trying to capture you."

"Who's Rokell?" asked Barney.

"You might say he's a mixed-up Gark."

Tibbo had talked about the Garks—the people of his

planet—when he was here in June, but he had never mentioned any of them by name.

"I thought all the Garks went back to Ornam last summer when you left."

"They did," agreed Tibbo. "But a new expedition is on the way to the moon. The first ships have already landed. Rokell was on one of them."

"Garks on the moon!" exclaimed Barney. "What are they doing there?"

"It's a good spot to study Mars and Venus. They're setting up a base on the far side of the moon."

"I know what you're doing!" cried Barney. "You're looking for another planet where you Garks can live because your sun is dying. You told me about that when you were here before."

"That's right," said Tibbo. "And you're the only person on Earth who knows about our plans. That's why Rokell is after you. He's afraid you'll talk about the Garks and get humans in a fighting mood."

"I wouldn't say anything against the Garks," protested Barney. "I know they're peaceful. Besides, no one would believe me if I told them I'd been talking to a Gark from Ornam. My own father and mother think I'm imagining it all."

"Sure. Any sensible Gark knows you're no danger to us. Rokell's the only one who's worried about you."

Barney groaned. "What's the matter with him?"

"It isn't all his fault. He was trained in defense. About five hundred years ago when he was a young man, the inhabitants of another planet attacked Ornam. So some Garks had to be taught to chase them off. You know, like an army. They were programed to hate anyone who wasn't a Gark. Rokell was in that army."

Barney thought this over. "Like in World War II we hated the Japanese. But we got over it."

"Most of our Garks returned to normal, too. But Rokell didn't. Unfortunately, he's dangerous. He wants to capture you and take you back to Ornam."

"Can't you make him leave me alone?" asked Barney. "You have a lot of power."

"Don't worry. I'm on my way to help you. Just be careful for three or four days."

"Three or four days!" cried Barney. "Rokell will get me before then!"

"Sorry. I can't do much for you till I get there. I can talk to you, but I can't be a lot of help at this distance. Be sure you're never alone and you'll be safe. Rokell doesn't want anyone to see him snatch you. That's why he pulled you toward the mountain."

"Oh, did Rokell make me float?"

"Right. If your mother hadn't called, he'd have whisked you up the mountain and taken you off in his spaceship. You'd have disappeared like a magician's rabbit."

There was a tap on the door, and Barney's father's voice asked, "Are you okay?"

"I'm fine!" Barney called.

"So long!" said Tibbo.

"Wait!" begged Barney. But Tibbo was gone.

Barney slid off the bed and went to the door. "Come in, Dad."

Finn darted in first and jumped onto the bed.

Barney's father looked around the room as if searching for something. "Do you have a visitor?"

Barney hedged. "No one's here now."

"There was someone?"

The boy nodded.

"Where'd he go?"

"Look, Dad." Barney drew in a deep breath and eased himself onto the edge of the bed. He sat there for a moment, scratching Finn's head and trying to figure out what to say. He couldn't think of any answer but the truth. "Tibbo was here. At least his voice was."

His father came over and sat down beside him. "Why do you keep imagining these things?" He looked worried.

"I'm not imagining them. The Garks are on the moon, and one of them—his name's Rokell—wants to capture me and take me to Ornam."

His father got up and walked away a few steps with his shoulders slumped. Then he turned back and said,

39

"The game's almost over, but if you come down now you'll be in time to catch the last few minutes of play."

The hockey game no longer seemed important. Slowly Barney followed his father and Finn downstairs, feeling lower than ever. It was no use telling his parents any more about people from space. They wouldn't believe him.

Later that evening he overheard his father talking with his mother. He caught the words *Barney* and *appointment with the doctor*.

I'll have to play it cool from now on, he thought. He certainly didn't want to go to the doctor when he wasn't even sick. But he had to share all this with someone. He shivered as he remembered the unseen power that had drawn him toward the mountain. Tibbo wasn't kidding. Rokell *was* dangerous. Any time now he could take him away, and there should be someone who'd know what had happened to him.

Of course he could tell Scott, but Scott was too young. Besides, he was already worried about Tibbo. If he heard about Rokell, he'd be having nightmares.

Dick wouldn't understand because he had forgotten all about Tibbo and the UFO.

There was one other person, though, who remembered. Kara.

6 Ø

Rokell Comes Again

When Barney went upstairs to get ready for bed, he was sure Tibbo would talk to him again that night, even though he was still millions of miles away.

He stood at the window and stared out at the countryside. There was no moon, but because of the snow he could see the steep white slope of Mount Casper with dark patches marking the woodlands.

The top of the mountain was silver against the star-dotted sky. Somewhere in that sky was his enemy, Rokell, the Gark who wanted to capture him. Probably he was hovering in a spaceship right now, waiting his chance.

Barney shuddered and pulled the drapes across the window. Not that anything like drapes would keep Rokell from finding him. Garks were thousands of years ahead of Earth in science, and with their scanners could zero in on a person right through the roof of a house or any place.

Tibbo had said to stay near people because Rokell wouldn't want a witness when he kidnapped him.

I'm alone in my room now, thought Barney. But if Rokell tries to take me, I'll yell, and Mom and Dad will come in a hurry. This was a consoling thought, but deep down he suspected that, if the Gark were desperate enough, nothing would stop him.

If only he could hear Tibbo's voice again! There were so many things he wanted to know. For one, why couldn't his parents and Dick remember about Tibbo, and the UFO—the spaceship—that had landed here last summer?

When Barney was in bed, he lay a long time, waiting for the tingle of his skin that meant Tibbo was watching him. Nothing happened. Even in the night he awakened, hoping to hear the space boy.

Tibbo had said he'd be here in person in two or three days. How was that possible? He had been traveling toward Ornam for six months. How could he get back to Earth in two or three days?

The next day was Monday, the beginning of a full week of vacation from school. Barney, tired from his restless night, slept late, and was still only half awake when Scott padded into his room at eight o'clock.

Barney lay motionless with his eyes closed, even though he could feel the little boy's breath on his cheek.

But when Scott whispered, "Are you awake?" Barney pounced on him and said, "Yes, and I'm going to get you for waking me up!"

Scott squealed delightedly and climbed on top of his brother.

"Hey, Barney, did you float again?"

"No. But I heard from Tibbo. He's on his way back here."

"What's he want this time?" asked Scott. There was fear in his voice.

"Just a friendly visit," answered Barney, hoping to reassure his brother. That was the truth, he told himself. It *was* friendly of Tibbo to travel so far to help him.

After breakfast he phoned Kara. "Want to go skiing? I'd like to talk to you about Tibbo."

Kara seemed pleased. "I'll meet you halfway."

"Great," said Barney. "I'll leave here at nine-thirty." The MacDougalls' home, a quarter of a mile to the east, was the nearest house to Crandalls. If he and Kara both left home at the same time, he'd be alone only three or four minutes before she came in sight.

But at fifteen minutes after nine, his mother called up the stairs, "I'm taking Scott for his dentist appointment now. Do you want to go along for the ride?"

In a panic Barney leaped from the chair where he had been reading. "No!" he shouted. "I'm going skiing with Kara. Can you wait a few minutes? I'll go out when you do." Wouldn't Rokell love to catch him alone in the house!

"Sorry. We'll just make it if we leave right away."

"I'm coming!" cried Barney.

He dived into his clothes closet for his ski boots and pulled them on. Then, still racing, he ran downstairs to gather up his skis, poles, jacket, and mitts.

"What's the rush?" asked his mother. "Just lock the door when you go."

"I'd rather leave when you do," he panted.

She looked puzzled, but said only, "I'll get the car out."

When Barney left the house with his mother and Scott, it was twenty-five minutes after nine. That was only five minutes ahead of schedule. Maybe Kara was getting an early start, too. If he'd had time he would have phoned her. Anyway, he encouraged himself, there'd be traffic going past all the time.

Barney watched his mother turn left from the driveway and start down Mount Casper Road toward the village. Then he headed right toward MacDougalls.

He was scarcely out of the driveway when a car passed him but, after that, he saw no more from either direction. Yesterday, when he had gone to Dick's, there had been a steady line. Where was everyone today?

Although the deserted road and the empty countryside

made him uneasy, he hurried on, giving a strong thrust with the forward ski at each step. Kara should come into sight soon.

But the minutes crawled on, and still he was the only creature moving on the snowy fields.

Stay near people. Tibbo's warning echoed in his ears.

For a moment Barney slowed his pace, wondering if he should go back home. But it would be just as dangerous to be alone there. Walls wouldn't stop Rokell.

Glancing up, he noted that the sky was clear, except for a small cloud that sat like a crown on top of Mount Casper. At least there wasn't any spaceship in sight.

He rounded a curve. Now his home was cut off from his view and, because of a small hill, he still couldn't see Kara or the house where she lived.

No cars passed. The silence was eerie.

Suddenly Barney felt his skin prickle. Tibbo! Now he felt safer.

But the voice that reached him was faint.

"Speed up, Barney! Guess who's in that cloud!"

Feeling like a chipmunk with a hawk overhead, Barney cast an anxious look at the cloud. As he pushed forward faster than ever, he panted, "Rokell?"

"Of course." Tibbo sounded cross. "I told you not to be alone."

All at once skiing became easier. At first Barney was pleased at how fast he was going. At this rate he'd be at

Kara's before Rokell had a chance to reach him.

Then he noticed he was no longer traveling beside the road. His skis had turned to the right and were taking him toward Mount Casper. Barney's joy disappeared like a melted snowball.

Tibbo's voice, far away, urged, "Fight!"

"Fight! Ha!" muttered Barney. No matter how he tried to change his direction, he was skimming faster and faster to the south across the open field. Soon he was floating inches above the snow with the tails of his skis hanging down.

"Tibbo! Help me!" he shouted.

"I can't!" Tibbo's voice was frantic. "I'm too far away."

"Barney!"

The call came from behind him. With an effort Barney managed to turn his head in the direction of the sound.

There was Kara, skiing toward him, her brown hair flying.

"Come back!" she screamed.

As if by magic, Barney dropped to the ground with a jolt that buried his skis deep in the powdery snow.

He still had his poles and, balancing with them, he managed to pull his skis to the surface. By the time he had turned around, Kara was near at hand.

She drew in several deep breaths before she could speak. "Barney!" she exclaimed. "What happened?"

She came closer. "I saw you going through the air. You were floating, just like you said. Your skis were hanging down."

He stared at her with a dazed feeling, and when he spoke, he was hoarse. "I'm—glad you came." His knees felt weak, as if they might not hold him up.

Standing beside Kara in the snow, his panic eased and he told her about Tibbo's warning.

"So I'm not supposed to be alone," he said unhappily. "How am I going to do that? I can't be with people all the time."

"I'll help," offered Kara.

Barney was suddenly aware that she was shivering. "You won't be able to do much if you freeze to death."

"I'm not cold." Her teeth were clicking together as she spoke. "I'm—just shaky. This is scary." Her direct brown eyes met his. "I'm not the only one. You're shaking, too."

"I guess I am," admitted Barney. "Let's get moving. Where'll we go?"

"To Dick's," she said promptly. "He'll want to help, too."

"But he doesn't—" began Barney.

Kara interrupted. "If I tell him what I just saw, he ought to believe, even if he doesn't remember about Tibbo."

Barney felt a warm flicker of hope. "You're right. Let's go!"

7 Ø

Mystery of the Fallen Trees

As Barney skied back along the road toward Pineville with Kara, he asked, "Have you seen any cars go by?"

"No, I'm sure I haven't."

"That's funny. I wonder—"

"What do you mean, you wonder?" asked Kara.

"I suppose it's a crazy idea, but usually there are cars on the road. If there had been any when I started floating across the fields, someone might've noticed me."

"Yeah—I see." Kara gazed toward the empty road and then back at Barney. "You think Rokell stopped the cars?"

Barney nodded. "He had the scene set this time, and I bet he's fighting mad that you showed up."

He turned and looked up at Mount Casper. The cloud that had rested on the peak was gone. He was quite sure Rokell's spaceship had been in that cloud. The Gark

50

must've given up for now. But when would he strike again?

Barney had gone only a short distance down the road with Kara when he felt the prickling of his skin.

"Tibbo's here!" he said. "Maybe he'll talk to both of us."

"Oh, no, I won't!" Tibbo said flatly. "One human is all I have time to look after."

"You ought to let Kara hear you. She just saved me from Rokell."

"I know that, and besides I like her," said Tibbo. "But you're the only one I talk to. And that's final."

Barney chuckled and explained to Kara. "He says he likes you, but he still won't talk to anyone but me. So if you don't mind, I'll find out what I can from him and then tell you about it afterward."

Tibbo was speaking again. "I'll be on the moon in a couple of days."

"That may be too late for me," said Barney. "You saw what Rokell just tried to do."

"I saw."

"I never know when he's around," complained Barney. "I don't even feel any prickles when he's coming."

Tibbo said, "Of course not. Rokell doesn't look into your mind. I do. That's why you feel the prickles when I come. And don't cry on *my* shoulder. Prickles or no

51

prickles, you'd be safe if you did what I said. I told you not to be—''

"Okay, okay," interrupted Barney. "I know what I have to do, but it isn't easy." Not wanting another lecture, he changed the subject. "You've been traveling away from Earth for six months. How can you get back so soon?"

"Science, my dear friend. The Garks have discovered how to travel faster than the speed of light."

"That's impossible! My friend Dick says Einstein proved it can't be done."

"Nothing's impossible to a Gark." Tibbo sounded smug. "Did you ever hear of tachyons?"

"No," said Barney.

"Some of your Earth scientists have, but they don't know what to do with them. Tachyons are tiny particles that move faster than anything yet discovered. And we've learned to harness them."

"Wow!"

"Wow is right. It's hard to navigate at this speed. It'd be easy to whap a star or plow right into the moon."

"Yeah? Don't put any dents in our moon," warned Barney. "How come you Garks are thinking about moving to Mars or Venus? Don't you have any planets near Ornam that'd be just as good?"

"I suppose you think we haven't looked!" said Tibbo in a cross tone. "All the good worlds are occupied. Like

52

Earth. It would be fine for us, but it's full of humans. And even if there were room for us, too, it wouldn't work. Garks are a lot different from you Earth people. You have trouble now with different colors and languages and religions. What if you added different shapes!''

"Oh, I guess you're right," said Barney. "You can cross off Mars and Venus, too. Our space probes have already checked them out. You couldn't live on them.''

"Not the way they are now, but we can change them, Earth boy," Tibbo said. "We have to find a place soon. I told you our sun is dying, and when that happens it gets bigger and hotter. In about three thousand years we'll have to leave Ornam or get fried.''

All the while Barney was talking with Tibbo, he was skiing along beside Kara. Now and then she glanced at him, clearly interested in his side of the conversation.

"How come my parents and Dick can't remember you, Tibbo?" demanded Barney.

"Rokell wiped out their memories. He overlooked Kara and Scott. Kara never saw the spaceship, you know, and Rokell didn't even realize she knew about me. I guess he thought Scott was too young to bother with.''

"What about me?" Barney asked. "Why doesn't he just make me forget? Then he won't have to worry about my spreading the word against the Garks.''

53

"He can't. Your memories go too deep. After all, you and I talked to each other a lot and we're friends. It's hard to make someone forget a friend. Whoops!" Tibbo's voice faded, then came back strongly. "Someone wants to use the scanner. Good luck with Dick."

The prickles were gone.

"Tibbo left," Barney informed Kara.

"Look!" She pointed down the road ahead of them. "I didn't want to bother you when you were talking to Tibbo, but something's going on down there. See that car in the road? And there are a lot of other cars behind it."

In the left traffic lane a highway truck with flashing lights was approaching the head of the line of parked vehicles. Soon Barney and Kara were close enough to see what had stopped traffic. A large tree had fallen across the road, blocking it completely.

"So that's why we didn't see any cars coming from this direction," remarked Barney. "I wonder why none came from the other way?"

"And I wonder why the tree came down? It hasn't been windy," Kara observed.

Barney paused. "Did you notice if Mom's car was in the driveway when we passed my house?"

"It wasn't, and it wasn't in the garage, either. The door was open."

"That means the tree didn't fall until after she and

54

Scott went past," Barney said. "Rokell must have timed it so they couldn't get back home to help me."

When he and Kara reached the tree, the highway crew were already at work with their chain saws.

As they went on toward Dick's, Barney told Kara about his conversation with Tibbo.

"He said Rokell wiped out my parents' memories and Dick's, but he overlooked you and Scott," said Barney.

"So that's what happened." Kara stopped skiing to consider this new information.

Barney nodded. "It's true, as Tibbo said. Rokell does make mistakes."

At the Williams house, Dick met them at the door with a book in his hand.

"Hey, great! Come on in. I was just thinking about making some hot chocolate."

Sitting around the kitchen table, drinking the hot chocolate and eating chocolate chip cookies, Barney and Kara told what had happened that morning.

At first Dick shook his head in complete disbelief. "You're pulling my leg," he complained. "What you say Barney did is against the laws of nature. People can't go up like balloons. Gravity holds us down."

"Listen," Kara insisted. "I *saw* Barney floating through the air. The ends of his skis were hanging down. And when I called to him he dropped like—like a stone."

55

Dick's right eyebrow went up and he looked sideways at Kara. His expression was skeptical, but he said, "Go on."

Kara continued earnestly, "There's something else that was funny. I saw one car when I first left the house, and after that I didn't see any in either direction."

"That's right," agreed Barney.

"The tree fell down," Dick reminded them. "Of course the cars couldn't get past."

"But why did the tree fall without any wind?" demanded Barney. "And why didn't cars come from the other direction?"

Dick stared at him thoughtfully. Then he looked at the kitchen clock. "It's almost news time." He leaped up and snapped on the kitchen radio. "There might be something about it on the Pineville station."

The blocked road was the first item of news.

"Traffic was held up for an hour this morning on Mount Casper Road," began the announcer. "By a strange coincidence, trees dropped across the road at two points a mile and a half apart at about the same time, bringing traffic to a standstill."

Barney and Kara exchanged triumphant glances. Dick looked thoughtful and held up his hand as if afraid they might interrupt the broadcast.

"In the absence of wind," the announcer continued, "police are baffled and are investigating to find out if the trees were felled deliberately. To add to the mystery, bystanders and highway crews report that not only were there no axe or saw marks on the tree trunks but also no footprints were found in the neighborhood of the two fallen trees.''

"How about that!" exclaimed Barney.

Dick and Kara both motioned him to silence.

The announcer was concluding the report. "No one was injured in the freak mishap, and traffic is now flowing freely on Mount Casper Road."

A commercial took over and Dick turned off the radio.

He came back and sat down opposite Barney and Kara. "Let's go look at what's left of the tree at this end of the road," he suggested.

"Let's!" Kara jumped to her feet and carried two of the mugs to the sink.

Barney looked across at Dick, trying to read his friend's thoughts. Dick was a logical thinker. He wanted proof before he'd believe in something as strange as this.

"Anyway, you're interested," said Barney.

"Right." Dick pushed back his chair. "If there's no scientific explanation why those trees came down, I might believe your wild story about that Gark."

Kara came back to the table. "And if it turns out a tornado blew them over, or something?"

Dick said firmly, "Then I'm still ready to stand by Barney and help make sure he's never alone until he feels safe again." He looked from Kara to Barney, his steady eyes confirming his promise. "Let's go check out that tree."

8 Ø

Barney's Bodyguards

Jagged splinters stood up from the stump of the fallen maple tree.

Two workmen were still at the site. The tree had been pulled to the side of the road and the men had already cut off the branches and stacked them in a huge pile. Now they were beginning to saw the trunk into logs.

One of the men noticed Kara and the boys examining the tree stump. He put down his saw and came over to talk to them.

"You know how this tree fell down?" he asked.

"Just heard it on the radio," said Dick. "I wanted to see if the stump looked rotten. I thought the tree might've dropped from old age."

"No way," said the workman. "That was a healthy tree. Look at those logs." He led them to the shoulder of the road and upended one of the cut pieces. "Solid."

"It'll make good firewood," remarked Barney, re-membering what his father had told him.

"Yeah," agreed the man. "I know a family that could use it. They're hard up right now. I think we can arrange for them to have this wood."

He retrieved his saw and returned to work.

Dick turned and looked at the stump. Then he surveyed the trees nearby. "Can't have been a tornado. It would've knocked down other trees."

He crossed the road with Barney and Kara.

"What do you think?" asked Barney.

"I think it's weird." Dick stopped, and all three maneuvered their skis so they could stand close together to talk, their shoulders hunched against the cold. "I gather you think Rokell engineered the falling of the trees to keep people away because he wanted to move you up Mount Casper to his spaceship."

Barney didn't hesitate. "Yes, that's what I think."

"Those Garks must have powers we don't have on Earth if they can do that to a tree without leaving any evidence."

"They're thousands of years ahead of us," Barney assured him.

"Their planet can't be in our solar system," Dick continued. "We're sure there's no intelligent life on any of the other planets around our sun. But other suns are so far away. How do the Garks get here?"

"They've learned to use tachyons for travel faster than the speed of light."

Dick said, "I've heard of tachyons, but last I knew no

one had ever seen one. Scientists aren't even sure they exist.'' He set his poles in the snow ahead of him. ''Ready, Kara? Shall we escort Barney home?''

''Oh, hey, you don't have to. Kara goes past my house anyway.'' Barney felt embarrassed.

''I know you don't need both of us, but I want to get in practice.'' Dick fell into place on one side of Barney and Kara on the other. ''We're your bodyguard, whether you like it or not. Sometimes the President and his family get tired of being shadowed by the Secret Service, but they have no choice. Same with you.''

Kara laughed. ''Rokell might as well give up.''

''I'm lucky to have you two,'' said Barney. ''Thanks. I hope you won't have to be on duty for long. Tibbo ought to get here in two or three days.''

''Now about tomorrow,'' said Dick. ''I'm supposed to go to my uncle's with my mother. He's the one who has the farm on Lake Tomega. How about coming with me, both of you? We can go ice skating on the lake. My uncle says it's frozen solid already.''

''I can't.'' Kara looked disappointed. ''My mother and I are going to Albany to buy me a new coat and see Grandma.'' Albany, the capital of New York State, was Pineville's nearest big shopping center.

''What about you, Barney?'' asked Dick.

''Sounds great. You sure it's all right with your aunt and uncle?''

''I'll ask Mom and let you know tonight.''

In spite of his narrow escape that morning, Barney felt his spirits soar. What could happen to him with two good friends like this!

Early that evening Dick called. The trip to his uncle's farm was all arranged.

Half an hour later Barney was getting his hockey stick from the closet when he felt the tingle of his skin.

"Hi, Tibbo," he said quietly. "Want to go ice skating tomorrow?" He dropped the stick onto the bed where he had already laid his warm cap and a woolen sweater.

"Ice skating!" Tibbo's voice followed him. "You're lucky you're not on the way to Ornam with Rokell. I told you not to be alone."

"Put it on tape. How many times do you have to say 'I told you so?' "

"Okay." Tibbo laughed. "You're right. Good thing for you Kara came along, though."

Barney started to close his bedroom door.

"Leave it open," said Tibbo. "No one will hear us. I've taken care of that. By the way, how come you humans can't talk with your mouth shut? We do it a lot on Ornam. We just broadcast our thoughts."

Barney sat down on his red chair in front of the shelves where he kept his books, his baseball trophy, a ship model he had made, and two hockey pucks. He had played ice hockey before his own parents had been killed in an accident two and a half years ago.

"Tibbo, did Rokell make those trees fall down?"

Tibbo sighed. "He did. But he forgot Kara might come along. He overlooks details."

"He doesn't seem like the usual Gark," said Barney. "You told me they're peaceful and don't want to do any harm to anyone."

"He's different, all right," agreed Tibbo. "I don't see why our leaders didn't reprogram him years ago. I wonder how he managed to hide his real feelings all this time. Of course, until he heard about you, he hadn't had any non-Garks to worry about for five hundred years."

"Is he a killer?"

"Oh, no. Not on purpose, anyway." Tibbo sounded concerned. "The trouble is he has such a one-track mind. He might kill by mistake."

"Why don't the Garks stop him now that they know what he's like?" asked Barney.

"They won't listen to me!" exploded Tibbo. "All they can think about is their moon landing. They keep saying, 'You look after Barney, Tibbo. You're the one who started talking to him.'"

"So that's the way it is. Okay, *you* get Rokell off my back, then!"

"I can't. I'm still millions of miles away. It'll be at least two more days before I can get there." His voice pleaded. "Be careful till I get back, Earth friend. So long, Barney."

Two more days before Tibbo would be near enough to

help him, thought Barney. Even with Kara and Dick standing guard, Rokell might succeed in capturing him before then.

Remembering the next day's trip, he felt more cheerful. He should be safe enough tomorrow at Lake Tomega with Dick.

One day at a time, he told himself. That's the way to do it. If he could stay out of Rokell's grasp tomorrow, he'd have just one more day to go until Tibbo arrived. Then *he* could do the worrying.

9 Ø

Trapped on the Ice

The east end of Lake Tomega, near Dick's uncle's farm, was almost clear of snow.

With large push brooms Dick and Barney swept the ice until it shone, then put on their skates.

A small campfire burned like an oasis of warmth on the snowy shore. Barney, seated on a log beside the fire, pulled his cap down over his ears and tightened his muffler against the cold, preparing to go onto the ice.

Just before he stood up, he glanced at the sky. It was a wintry blue with a few scattered clouds. One, a small, round cloud, was floating directly above Lake Tomega.

He watched it for a moment. Was it his imagination, or was it more stationary than the other clouds? It reminded him of the one that had sat on top of Mount Casper yesterday.

He was about to point it out to Dick but then decided—why harp on Rokell all the time? Dick must get sick of hearing about him, especially when he only half-believed in Garks.

It was great of Dick to agree to be a bodyguard, as he called it. Barney felt foolish letting his friends protect him this way, but he was grateful. It could make a life and death difference.

Dick was already on the ice, the skates making his legs look longer than ever. He was moving slowly, the way he did almost everything. Dick rarely hurried.

Barney hadn't been on skates for over a year, but a few minutes and two spills later it all came back to him. Pulling a puck from his pocket, he tossed it onto the ice.

He was chasing it around with his hockey stick when, without warning, another stick leaped in front of him and whacked the puck across the ice. Barney chuckled and gave chase as Dick shot after the flying disk in one of his rare fast moves. Barney's legs were not as long as Dick's, but his ability to pour on the speed and keep it on made it an equal contest.

Whacking the puck around was fun, but, deciding a game would be better, they roughly marked off a rink on the ice. Next they rolled four large balls of snow and placed two at each end of the rink to act as goalposts. If the puck went between the balls, it was a goal.

Each of the boys was a one-man team, and it made for fast play. Dick tired first and skated toward the bonfire which was still burning beside the lake. The score was Dick 6, Barney 7.

"You quitting?" asked Barney.

"I've had it, Superman," Dick panted. "Besides, it must be lunchtime and I'm starved."

"I'm going once around," said Barney. "Be right back."

"Take your time." Dick tossed a handful of sticks onto the fire and then sat down on the log beside it. He began to unlace his skates.

Barney started around the section of lake he and Dick had swept. It was large enough to give him a chance to build up speed. Bent at the waist in racing position, he sprinted around the ice as fast as he could go.

When he had completed the circle a few minutes later, Dick was putting on one of his snow boots in a leisurely way. The skate was still on his other foot. Obviously he had been dreaming or figuring out some scientific problem. That was like Dick, off in another world.

He glanced up at Barney. "Great form! Keep practicing!"

With a wave, Barney was off again. The wind whistled in his ears and his blades cut cleanly into the ice. As he sped along he imagined he was in a race with an Olympic competitor at his heels.

Halfway around the circle, some sound or motion made him look toward the fire. Dick was standing beside it, waving his arms. He seemed to be shouting, but Barney couldn't hear him. Next he pointed toward the farmhouse, out of sight on the far side of the little grove of trees that lay beyond the meadow. A moment later he turned away.

"Wait!" shouted Barney.

But Dick, already running across the snowy meadow, didn't seem to hear him. It was clear he had forgotten he was a bodyguard.

At once Barney realized his danger. If Rokell was up there in that cloud, he was waiting for a chance like this. Soon Dick would be out of sight among the trees. Already he was out of earshot.

Now Barney's race was in earnest. No more circling the end of the lake, daydreaming of world competition, but a desperate beeline race for shore.

The fears that stalked his mind drove him like a whip. If Rokell caught him and took him to Ornam, he might never return. At best, it would probably be years before he'd be able to come back.

The trip itself, traveling in a spaceship for months with a mixed-up Gark, would be worse than being a hostage. He didn't even know what a Gark looked like!

A shadow fell across the ice. The cloud. Rokell's cloud.

Barney's heart was a huge ache in his chest. Every breath he drew was sharp and painful, but he didn't let up his speed.

The cloud dropped lower, changing the morning

brightness to twilight. Lower and lower it came until it was only a few feet above his head.

Though Barney wanted to scream, he couldn't spare the breath.

Wisps of cloud floated down like ghosts, but he could still see the surface of the ice and beyond that the bonfire toward which he was skating. But even when he reached the shore he wouldn't be safe. How fast could he run with skates on? Rokell certainly wouldn't give him time to take them off.

What was that Gark waiting for? Perhaps he was holding off until Dick was in the woods.

Dick will feel terrible when he finds out I'm gone, thought Barney.

Suddenly all of his attention was riveted on one thing. Some distance ahead, but directly in front of him, a dark spot appeared in the ice. As he watched, it seemed to grow. Barney skated to the right to avoid it, but the spot expanded to the right. When he swerved left, the dark area stretched left.

Now he was close enough to confirm his worst doubts. The dark place was a hole. In some way Rokell had melted the ice. He had given up trying to take him to Ornam and was going to drown him!

10 Ø

A Leap for Life

Barney turned sharply to the left in a desperate effort to avoid the black hole and reach land. At first he thought he was going to make it.

A moment later he lost all hope when he felt Rokell's power take over his body. This time Barney didn't have a floating sensation. His skates continued to make contact with the ice, but he couldn't make them go where he wished. Against his will, he was speeding straight toward the opening in the ice.

He was within three or four feet of the hole when, without warning, he was again in control.

Taken by surprise, it seemed there was nothing he could do to save himself. It was too late to turn, and he was going too fast to stop. The black water rippled in front of him. Automatically he made the one possible move. He crouched low and jumped.

Sailing out above the water, he expected at any second to splash into it. But to his amazed relief, his skates grated on the far rim of the ice and he fell forward, still speeding, in a sprawling, belly-down slide that he thought would never end.

At last his momentum was spent and he sat up, unable to believe his good luck. When he looked back, the water still rippled but the hole was smaller than he had thought it was. It wasn't such a big thing to jump over a hole that size.

The sun was again gleaming on the ice and, looking up, Barney saw that the cloud had lifted. It was quite high now, and, as he watched, it rose with amazing speed until it disappeared completely.

Why did Rokell take off?

"Barney!"

A voice calling from the meadow made him turn. Dick, apparently breathless from running, was almost to the shore of the lake. Not stopping to put on his skates, he ran onto the ice and came slipping and sliding toward Barney.

"Are you all right?" he panted.

"I guess so." Barney struggled to his feet and brushed at the snow on the front of his jacket and pants. He could feel his heart jumping like an animal trapped inside his chest.

"What happened?" asked Dick. "I saw you skating and then you flew up in the air. I never saw a jump like

that, except once when I watched a trick skater go over a whole row of barrels.''

"Rokell tried to drown me!" said Barney. "I *had* to clear that hole in the ice." He turned around and pointed back. "See?" He stared at the hole, bewildered. "It's shrinking!"

"Where'd that come from?" asked Dick. "There wasn't any hole when I left." He approached it cautiously.

Barney followed him. The hole was getting smaller and smaller. "At this rate it'll be gone in a couple of minutes," he said. "It was a lot bigger than that when I went over it."

He and Dick stood side by side watching the blue-tinged ice around the edge of the hole come closer and closer together until, like a gaping black mouth shutting, the edges met. The water was gone from sight and only solid ice remained where the hole had been.

Dick let out an explosive breath. "Man!" He stepped gingerly onto the newly formed ice. Then, when it held firm, he stamped on it. "It's as solid as the rest of the lake." He shook his head as if bewildered. "Rokell could have made the hole with a laser beam, but I don't understand how he closed it up."

They went back to the fire and Barney dropped onto the log, glad to sit down.

"I owe you a big apology for leaving," said Dick. "My uncle came out and shouted to me to come in on

74

the double. Gramps was on the phone and wanted to talk to me. Well, I went. Long distance, you know, and I wanted to talk to him. I forgot about Rokell. And of course I didn't actually believe he was for real. I do now, though."

Barney looked up from unlacing his skates. "It's about time," he said with a grin. "How'd you get back here so fast?"

"I didn't go far—inside the woods maybe ten feet. Then I remembered I was on bodyguard duty. Some friend I am, I thought. And suppose you and Kara were right and you were in real danger. So I turned around and started back. Then when I saw that cloud over the lake I decided it didn't look normal, so I began to run. About that time the cloud began to go up in the air."

"Rokell must have seen you coming. I felt him let go of me when I was almost to the hole." Barney pulled off one of his skates. "So you saw me jump."

Dick nodded.

Barney looked down at the skate in his hand. "I don't know how I got across that hole. When I jumped, it looked like the Grand Canyon. Must be I made it because I had been pouring on the speed like the fellow you saw go over the barrels."

Dick said hoarsely, "I hate to think what could've happened. I swear I'll be your shadow till Rokell is gone."

"Thanks," said Barney. "Tibbo won't be back for a

couple of days. I hope I can hold on that long." He suddenly became aware of the minutes slipping by. "You're going to be in trouble for not getting to the phone."

Dick shrugged. "I know. And they'll never believe what happened."

When Barney and Dick reached the farmhouse, Dick's mother, his uncle, and aunt were at the table, eating lunch.

"What happened to you?" asked his uncle. "We kept Gramps on the line, waiting for you. I hate to think of his phone bill."

"I'm sorry, said Dick. "It was an emergency. Barney was in trouble and I had to help him."

"Oh?" Mrs. Williams looked up with a worried expression.

"He almost fell in a hole in the lake," Dick explained.

"A hole?" His uncle's voice came up sharply. "There aren't any holes in the ice. I wouldn't have let you go skating if there were. Where is it?"

"It isn't there now. You see"—Dick motioned Barney to a chair and then sat down across from him—"Barney's being chased by a—person from another planet, and this person—he's called a Gark—melted the ice and then he froze it up again."

His uncle glared at him. "Oh, come now!"

"Dick!" His mother's voice was reproachful.

Barney wished he could sink through the floor. This was terrible, getting his best friend into all this trouble.

"It's true." Barney's voice came out as a croak. He cleared his throat and went on. "Rokell's trying to take me to his planet, Ornam. He doesn't want—"

Dick's aunt broke in with her gentle voice. "Let's forget all about it now. The food's getting cold. Dick, pass your friend the mashed potatoes."

On their way home in the car, Barney and Dick tried to explain to Dick's mother, but she merely became more upset.

"I never heard such nonsense!" she said. "Barney, I've always thought you were a sensible boy."

Barney was in the back seat. "I am," he assured her. "I don't like having this Gark after me. I never had any trouble like this until Tibbo came last summer."

"Tibbo!" Mrs. Williams jerked the wheel, and Barney reached for the seat ahead of him to brace himself, expecting a crash.

She regained control of the wheel and rubbed her face with a trembling hand.

"Let's not talk about it now, Mom," suggested Dick. "I'm going to phone Gramps when I get home. I'll use my allowance to pay for the call."

"That's a nice idea," she said. "But don't start talking to him about the—the Garks."

11 Ø

Adrift in a Spaceship

It was almost dinnertime when Dick's mother dropped Barney off at home.

As soon as he opened the back door, Finn jumped all over him and Scott announced his latest news at the top of his voice.

"I got to know a new kid today!" he shouted. "Mom took me to the park and we slid down a big hill on the toboggan."

Barney stared at his brother, unable to understand what he was talking about. His thoughts were still back at Lake Tomega on the edge of the terrifying black hole in the ice.

Finally he managed to say, "That's great, Tiger."

This seemed to satisfy Scott, for he raced off, chasing Finn McCool up the steps.

Barney hung up his coat and left his skates and hockey stick in the back hall.

Still in a daze, he climbed heavily to the kitchen.

His mother asked, "How was it? Did you have a good time with Dick?"

He wanted to answer, "It was a terrible day. I almost drowned, and Dick's whole family think I'm off my rocker."

But the words didn't come out. He remembered too well his mother's sadness when he told her about floating in the air. If he tried to explain what had happened today, she'd be sure he had flipped and he'd be visiting the doctor the next morning.

He had to say something for she was looking at him inquiringly, waiting for his reply.

"Swell. It was swell," he said.

"Oh?" His mother gave him a glance that seemed to go through to his brain. "You don't sound very happy about it. What happened?"

Barney tried to act enthusiastic. "We played ice hockey, Dick and I. The ice was great, nice and smooth."

His father came into the kitchen in time to hear Barney's remark.

"Ice hockey for two. That's hard work. You're on the move every minute. Who won?"

"I did, by one point." He managed a grin and went on, feeling like an actor as he told about the day at Lake Tomega, making it sound like an ordinary outing. It was all true—with the most important parts left out. "Dick's aunt had a great lunch," he said. "It was more like Thanksgiving dinner. She had turkey and gravy and mince pie."

His mother laughed. "I suppose you don't feel like eating a bite tonight. We're having spaghetti and meatballs."

One of his favorite meals. But the very thought of eating made him feel sick. He had been so upset when he ate lunch, it was still like lead in his stomach.

"I'm sorry," he said. "Can you save some? I'll be hungry tomorrow."

Early that evening Barney was in his room, worrying about Rokell, when Dick phoned.

"Mom and Dad are out," he began, "so I thought I'd give you a call."

Barney's spirits took another drop. It must be bad if Dick had to wait until he was alone to talk with him.

"Everything's okay," Dick went on. "Mom and Dad hashed it all over, about the Garks and the hole in the ice and everything. They can't decide if we imagined it or made the whole thing up for an alibi so I wouldn't get jumped on for not getting to the phone to talk to Gramps."

"Did you tell them it was one-hundred-percent true?"

"Of course. But they don't believe in UFO's or visitors from other planets or anything like that. So finally I gave up.''

"I thought they might not want you to see me any more.''

"Nothing like that,'' Dick assured him. "They think you're swell. But don't try telling them about Rokell and the Garks.''

"Right. I'm not bringing the subject up at home, either.''

Dick asked, "Did you hear anything from Tibbo?''

"No.''

"I wonder why he didn't help when Rokell was after you today.''

"Yeah. I thought about that, too. Well, sometimes he can't get to the scanner. That's what he looks through to find me. Anyway, he ought to be here in another day.''

That night Barney was sound asleep when he was awakened by the tingle of his skin and a voice in his ears.

"Wake up, you lazy Earth boy. You have company.''

Barney sat up in bed. "Where are you?''

"Not as near as I thought I'd be. We're having problems with the tachyon system. We only traveled about a million miles today.''

"*Only* a million!'' exclaimed Barney. "That's a lot.''

"Not when we still have millions and millions to

go.'' Tibbo sounded gloomy. "I hope your luck holds out. I don't know when I'll get there. The way this ship's acting, it'll take weeks.''

Barney was shocked. "I'll never make it. Do you know what happened to me yesterday?''

"No. Everyone on this ship had to work. I didn't even get near the scanner.''

Barney quickly told him about his narrow escape.

"You said Rokell's not a killer,'' he finished indignantly. "But what would you call it when he tries to drown me?''

"You've got it wrong, Barney,'' Tibbo assured him. "I know what he was trying to do. You said his cloud was low over the lake?''

"Practically on top of my head.''

"He was going to have you skate to the edge of the hole, then he would swoop down and pick you up and take you into the spaceship. Your friends would see your skate marks at the edge of the hole and think you had drowned. But actually, you wouldn't even get your feet wet.''

"That may be what he planned,'' consented Barney. "But as soon as Dick came back out of the woods, Rokell moved off and left me practically on top of that hole, skating full steam ahead. If I hadn't made a flying leap, I'd have been done for.''

"He probably helped you jump.''

"No, he didn't." Barney was sure of that. "I could tell the minute he let go. And besides, he froze the ice right after I jumped. If I'd fallen in and he closed the hole, that would've been slightly fatal."

"*Hm*. You may be right." Tibbo sounded less sure of himself. "I told you Rokell overlooks details. No regular Gark would be so careless."

"Can't you do something to stop him?" asked Barney.

"If I were there, I could," Tibbo answered.

"Tell some of those Garks on the moon to keep Rokell busy," urged Barney.

"All right, I will," said Tibbo. "My best friend—my best Gark friend, that is, you're my best Earth friend—must be on the moon by now. I'll try to get a message through to him. His name's Naf."

"Naf," repeated Barney.

"I can't promise anything," Tibbo went on. "I might not be able to reach him." After a short silence, he said, "Barney, if anything happened to you, I'd feel terrible. But I might as well be honest. We're in trouble on this ship, even worse than I told you. Our power system has fizzled out. We can't even steer this craft. Drifting along the way we are, one of our own moonships might ram us, or we could get lost and float around in space for millions of years. We're running low on food and water and—"

Tibbo's voice cut off, and the prickles left Barney's skin.

"Tibbo!" The name burst from Barney's throat. Then, hearing the echo of his own voice, he was shocked into silence. Now that Tibbo had gone, sounds would carry to the other rooms.

Sure enough, his father called, "Barney, is that you?"

"Yes—I'm all right. I guess—I had a bad dream."

A bad dream. It was a nightmare, he thought. Poor Tibbo! How awful to float around in space! And as for himself, if Tibbo was lost, so was he. He didn't know anyone else who had enough power to fight Rokell. No use counting on Naf. Tibbo hadn't had a chance to contact him.

12 Ø

Dark Future

Two paws pressed down on Barney's chest and a wet tongue slapped at his chin.

"Hey, Finn!" Barney, now wide awake, seized his dog around the neck and wrestled with him. Finn shook himself loose, then took hold of the covers with his teeth and pulled.

"Don't do that!" cried Barney. "I have to make this bed!"

Scott was eating oatmeal with brown sugar on it when Barney went down to the kitchen.

"Want to go to the park with me and Mom?" he asked. "Maybe my friend will be there and you can see him."

"Sounds great," said Barney. To his surprise, a day on a toboggan with Scott was just what he wanted.

"Don't promise too fast," said his mother. "Your friend Dick phoned. He's going to Albany with his mother to get new slacks for school. He wants to know if you'd like to go along."

Dick's a swell guy! thought Barney. He's making sure I don't get left alone with Rokell.

Aloud he said, "I'd rather go with you and Scott." He hated shopping trips.

"Fine," said his mother. "As soon as I clear up the breakfast dishes and make a pudding for dinner, I'll be ready to go."

Again Barney surprised himself by saying, "I'll take care of the dishes."

As he scraped the plates and stacked them in the dishwasher, his mind was busy, facing reality. He hadn't suddenly become perfect. The truth was that he was more and more sure he couldn't escape Rokell.

It might be days—or weeks—before Tibbo could help him, if ever. The way he had broken off in the middle of a sentence last night made Barney afraid his friend's spaceship had already crashed.

Every now and then he felt sick with fear, realizing that he might be snatched up and taken to Ornam at any time. That he might never again see his parents, or Dick—or Scott. The hardest one of all to leave was Scott. So time spent with his brother was important.

Now that he had figured this out, he began to wonder what else he could do to show his mother how much he appreciated her.

When he had taken care of the dishes, he ran upstairs

and made his bed. This time he didn't do a quick cover job with the bedspread. Instead, he removed Finn's rubber ball, a hockey puck, his pajamas, and a pair of shoes. Then he smoothed the sheets and straightened the rumpled blankets. His mother stopped in the doorway as he was adding the bedspread to his masterpiece.

She came closer. "I can't believe it!"

Barney made a big production out of removing the last wrinkle. "I'll take Finn out before we go."

By the time they reached the park, the hillside was already dotted with children on sleds, toboggans, and plastic skimmers.

As soon as the car stopped, Scott leaped out, shouting, "There's my friend Nickie!" He ran toward a small boy in a red parka who was smashing a handful of snow into the face of another little boy.

"That Nickie's a terror," said Barney's mother, "but Scott thinks he's wonderful. I hope he doesn't get any ideas from him."

Still in his helpful mood, Barney offered to take care of the two little boys while their mothers went shopping. On the first ride down the hill, Barney knew he'd taken on a big job. Nickie kept showing off, and Scott thought everything he did was funny and laughed at him.

The sky soon became overcast and a few flakes of snow drifted through the air. Gradually the crowd in the park thinned.

Coming up the hill for the fourth time, towing the

toboggan, Barney couldn't help wondering if Rokell would try something now that there were only a few children as witnesses.

Just then Nickie pushed Scott in front of an oncoming sled and Barney had to leap to save him. With Nickie around he had no time to worry and, to Barney's relief, there was no sign of the Gark that afternoon.

In the evening Dick called.

"Hey, Barney," he said. "Every time I phone you I hold my breath till you answer. I'm always afraid I'll hear you've disappeared."

"Not yet. But if I do, you tell Mom and Dad what's happened, will you?"

"Sure. Say, did you read the paper last night?"

"No. Why?"

"The Pineville Ski Club is having an all day cross-country ski trip tomorrow. Any fairly good skier can go. We take our own sandwiches."

All day outdoors with friends. It sounded great to Barney, and since there'd be many people along, he should be safe from Rokell.

"I'll ask," he said, "but I'm sure I can go."

"All right. You check, and I'll call Kara."

At nine the next morning, Mrs. MacDougall dropped Barney, Dick, and Kara off several miles west of Pineville at the starting point for the cross-country trip.

The leader, Mr. Yost, a physical education teacher from Pineville High, called for attention and explained, "We stay together, following the red flags that mark the route. We end up back at Pineville some time this afternoon, depending on how fast we go. Sign your name and phone number on this sheet so we know who's on this trip. Whatever you do, don't wander off by yourselves. We don't want to send out a search party."

At the start, the three friends were in the middle of the group. After a solid night's sleep, Barney felt good. He was sure he was in no danger today, even though Tibbo wasn't nearby. What could happen to him in this crowd?

In spite of his confidence, he glanced up at the sky. A small cloud was overhead. But, determined not to suspect Rokell was in every cloud, Barney fell into a comfortable stride. Today he was going to forget the dangerous Gark.

13

Cliff Ahead

Soon the nineteen skiers were stretched out in a long, narrow line behind the leader, Mr. Yost.

Following the floor of the valley, they crossed fields and frozen brooks and slid single file through woodlands.

Whenever the way was open, Barney skied beside his friends. He liked the quick, light way Kara moved. A picture of her with her knee-high gaiters and her dark hair topped with the red cap would make a good ski commercial.

No one would use Dick for an advertisement, though. Rambling along on his skinny legs, straight mousebrown hair flying above green earmuffs, he didn't have much style. But Barney knew from experience that Dick could travel at that lazy-looking pace of his for hours.

By ten-thirty the skiing party had reached the end of the valley where one mountain range folded into another.

For the next hour they continued to rise, but always on an easy grade.

"Yost did a great job mapping out this trip," said Dick when they stopped for a rest. He motioned to the valley far below. "I must've climbed all the way, but I didn't know I was doing it."

Since the start of the trip, Barney hadn't seen a cloud shadow, but now he couldn't resist scanning the sky. It was completely clear. Rokell must have given up.

They continued their gradual climb, with a brief stop for lunch, until suddenly they came out from behind a peak onto a plateau.

Mr. Yost called a halt. "This is as high as we go." His mittened hand pointed down the shining white slope, unmarked by any tracks, except for the flags the teacher had placed a few days before. "There's the end of our tour."

Barney followed the direction of his hand, down, down to the valley, where the village of Pineville looked like the collection of toy houses on Scott's electric train layout. Staring at the incline, he took out his handkerchief and wiped the fine snow from his sunglasses. This hill was a small one compared with Mount Casper, yet it looked like a long way down.

Kara came up beside him. "How are we going to ski down *there?*"

Barney wondered the same thing.

All around him people were exclaiming nervously about the slope. He heard one woman complain, "This isn't my idea of a cross-country trip."

"Don't get all shook up," said Mr. Yost, skiing to the front of the group. "It isn't as bad as you think. Look, it's like a series of small hills with flat spots between them. I went over this whole route with some friends who are just average cross-country skiers, and no one had any problems."

Barney studied the hillside again. Yes, he could see what Mr. Yost meant. He didn't know about the others in the party, but if all the little hills were like the first one, he and his two friends would have no trouble. Besides, Mr. Yost had a reputation for knowing what he was doing.

Barney glanced at Kara and she smiled back at him and nodded.

Dick came closer to them. "I know this place. Do you remember it, Barney?"

Barney studied the fall of land in front of him. On the right was a line of pine trees and farther down, off to the left, a cluster of bushes.

"Yeah . . ." he said slowly. "There's a cliff way down there on the other side of those bushes."

"That's it." Dick, shivering and shuffling around on his skis, wrapped his long arms around his chest. "We climbed here last fall."

"That cliff is straight up and down," Barney told Kara, "with rocks at the bottom, a long way down. You'd need wings to go over it."

Kara shuddered. "I'll stay with this roller coaster ahead of us."

In spite of the strong wind from the north that was chilling everyone, Mr. Yost took time to explain the descent.

He finished by saying, "Just follow me. Don't go off to the left past the flags." He pointed to the red flags he had used to mark the trail. "When you get to the bottom, it's only a short run to Pineville. Everyone all set?"

No one objected, so he pushed off down the slope. At the first level spot he stopped and waited. It looked easy, thought Barney.

Dick skied over to him. "You're trailing a shoelace."

Barney took off his mitts and crouched to tie the strings. When he pulled them tight, one broke in his hand.

The skiers were beginning to stream down the hillside. Dick and Kara were waiting for him.

Barney's fingers, stiff with cold, had trouble tying the two pieces together.

Kara saw his problem and unzipped her rucksack, saying, "I have an extra pair of strings."

Almost everyone was gone now. The last two, a man

and woman, paused on the first level area and called back to them.

"Having trouble? Need any help?"

"Broken shoestring!" shouted Dick. "No, we have a spare. Thanks, go ahead!"

By the time Barney had the new lace threaded and tied, he was alone on the hill with Kara and Dick.

"Sorry to hold you up," he said. "Thanks for waiting."

For the first time since he had left the starting point, he noticed a cloud overhead. It immediately worried him.

He clutched his ski poles. "Let's go!"

Dick's head was tilted back, and Barney knew he, too, had seen the cloud.

"Stay close," warned Dick.

Barney gave a quick nod. "You can depend on it."

The three started down side by side with Dick on Barney's right and Kara on his left. The sun made the snow sparkle like icicles on a Christmas tree. The slope was not too difficult, even for cross-country skis. All in a row, they reached the first level space.

Again Barney looked up. The cloud was directly overhead. Had it traveled with them, or did it just seem that way?

The three friends left the flat area in the same order as before, but they had gone only a short distance when

94

Barney noticed that he and Kara were drifting to the left, away from Dick. He motioned her to move to the right, intending to go that way, too. But to his horror, his skis remained pointed toward the left as if a magnet were pulling them. Already he had passed the red flags that marked the route. If he continued like this, he'd go through the clump of bushes and down the hill toward the cliff.

Kara was still on his left, skiing in the same direction as he. She turned frightened eyes to him.

"Go over to Dick!" he shouted.

Her answer shocked him. "I can't!"

This was worse than ever before. Rokell was taking him over the cliff, and it looked as if he was taking Kara over it, too.

14 Ø

Buried In Snow

The gap between Barney and Dick widened.

Wanting his friend to know what was happening to him and Kara, Barney shouted, "Rokell has us!"

The tall, lean figure continued down the hill.

Barney tried again. "Dick!"

This time Dick's head snapped toward the sound. He straightened and then jerked his skis to the left.

Desperately, Barney waved him away. "Go back!" No one else must go over the cliff.

Dick still sped toward him and Kara.

"Go back!" Barney cried again. "Get help! It's Rokell."

Suddenly Dick snowplowed to a halt and stared back up the slope. Pointing to the top, he shouted something Barney couldn't hear. Then he turned around and skied rapidly downhill after Mr. Yost's group.

Good! thought Barney. He didn't know what Dick

had seen, but at least he'd be alive to tell everyone why he and Kara had gone over the cliff.

The sound of screaming reached his ears, and at first he thought it was his own voice. Then, managing to glance toward Kara, he saw her mouth open and knew it was her cry he had heard. She knew exactly what was ahead and was screaming her protest.

Seeing her beside him, traveling toward the same terrible end as he, Barney rebelled. No Gark was going to kill them. He'd fall in front of her and bring both of them to the ground.

With a quick motion, he flung himself toward her. To his despair, he only toppled over part of the way, then popped up like a weighted toy. He tried again. This time he felt as if he were in a steel vise. He couldn't move his body in any direction.

No matter how he tried to stop himself or change course, he continued to speed down the hill like a comet, knees bent, head into the wind. Although he was skiing like a professional, he took no pride in it, aware it wasn't because of his own skill. That Gark—Rokell— was controlling him like a puppet.

"Tibbo! Help us!" cried Barney.

The wind rushing past was his only answer. Tibbo must still be working to get the spaceship repaired or, worse, already be dead in a crash with a moonship.

Just ahead was the cluster of bushes that had helped

him recognize this area. Surely they'd slow him and Kara down. But no, the wiry branches seemed as pliable as grass when they skimmed through.

Beyond the bushes was a steep hill, ending at the cliff. Still in Rokell's grip, the two skiers entered the slope at the halfway point on a course that aimed them straight toward a great curling lip of snow beyond which the land disappeared. Far below, in the distance, Barney could see the thread of road that wound the length of the valley.

A rumbling noise reached his ears. Within seconds it became louder.

But Barney, streaking helplessly toward the dropoff, had little time to wonder about distant sounds. Particles of snow stung his face like coarse sandpaper, and the wind was so strong it took his breath away. Strangest of all, the ground under his feet seemed to be traveling with him.

The overhang of snow, now only fifty feet ahead, suddenly leaped away from him. On and on it sped, with the snow from the hillside going with it like a great, moving beltway.

Barney knew by now he and Kara must have passed the edge of the cliff but they hadn't fallen, and that curl of snow was still ahead of them.

Through his daze of fear, the truth reached his mind. That rumbling sound was a snowslide. All the snow on this hillside was coming down, and he and Kara were riding on top of it!

Barney's body was imprisoned, but his mind was free, leaping from idea to idea.

What did Rokell plan to do? At any moment Barney expected the Gark to snatch him into his spaceship. Or would he let him fall to his death?

And what would happen to Kara?

Rokell must have started the sliding snow, but why had he done it? wondered Barney. Whatever the reason, it was a magic carpet. Without it, he and Kara would already have crashed to the ground.

At first the snow had shot straight out over the cliff, but now it was dropping fast. Without any effort of his own, Barney found himself crouching low. Ahead of him, the curling lip that had been at the edge of the cliff vanished.

He was still high above the ground, so whether he wanted to or not, he was making a jump. As the snow fell away beneath him, Barney felt his body straighten and lean forward over his skis in exact imitation of Olympic jumpers he had seen on TV.

So far, so good. Already he must be past the rocks at the base of the cliff. He couldn't see Kara, but she must be close behind him. If only Rokell would help both of them sail far enough so they wouldn't be buried under the snowslide. . . .

For seconds Barney was airborne. Then the ground came toward him with lightning speed. Though he landed on his feet, his skis shot out from under him and he slid down the incline on his back, his skis waving in the air.

Behind him he could hear the thud of the snow from the hillside hitting the ground, but only a few clumps rolled harmlessly past him. The air filled with snowmist. Terror stricken, he wondered: Was Kara back there?

Finally he was able to stop his slide. He sat up and shouted, "Kara!"

Again and again he yelled as loud as he could, while with frantic fingers he unfastened his skis. Then he scrambled to his feet.

As he stood up he caught a glimpse of the ski group hurrying toward him. They seemed to be moving fast, but he was afraid they might not be in time to save Kara.

Whirling around, he searched the rough snow.

His sunglasses were gone, and he squinted into the dazzling light. His eyes raked across the tumbled white mounds, hoping to see a movement, or something that would tell him where Kara was.

A flash of red was his first clue. He ran and crawled and climbed toward the red beacon. At last he snatched up the red cap. Although it was Kara's, she was no place in sight. Falling to his knees, he began to dig, but the snow at that point was so solid he could make little headway. She *couldn't* be under that.

Straightening, he called again. No answer. But as he studied the rough heaps of snow to the north, farther from the base of the cliff, something showed dark amid the white. Something that looked like a stick standing upright.

Barney jumped to his feet and struggled toward the thin black finger, losing sight of it behind an unusually large mound but finding it again a second later.

As he drew nearer, the snow became softer and more powdery, and he sank to his knees with each step.

At last he reached his goal and knew what the black stick was. It was a ski, the tip of a ski, projecting from the snow. It had to be Kara's. Was she under there? And if she was, could she possibly be alive?

15 Ø

A Girl Like Wax

Barney dug around the point of the ski, making the snow fly as if he were a dog searching for a bone.

Soon he came to a foot, Kara's foot, with the boot firmly clamped to the ski. The position of the ski and her foot told him she must be on her back.

He didn't take the time to uncover the rest of her leg but instead worked rapidly toward her head, digging so fast the perspiration rolled down his face in spite of the cold. When he discovered she was in a half-sitting position, his hopes rose. That meant her head must be close to the surface.

Soon, only twelve inches down, he sighted the top of her head. Seconds later he broke into a small cave where her breath had melted the snow.

Her eyes were closed and she lay as still as if she were made of wax.

"Kara!" shouted Barney. He was so full of fear his heart throbbed in his throat. "Wake up!"

She made no answer, and her black lashes rested motionless on her cheeks.

Barney pulled off his glove and felt her face. Even to his chilled fingers it was cold, but then it would be, after being buried in the snow. He held his hand near her nose and was quite sure he felt a warm stirring of breath. Leaning back, he could see a mist as her breath hit the cold air.

She was alive!

Refreshed by hope, he fell to work again, digging the snow away from her body. As he dug, every now and then he called her name and scanned her face, hoping to see her eyes open.

Why had Rokell pulled her over the cliff? Was the Gark still hovering nearby, planning to grab both of them? So far Barney hadn't even taken the time to search for the cloud that had been overhead. Now, snatching a quick upward look, he saw only a clear blue sky. That, at least, was good, he thought, as he continued to claw at the snow.

By the time Mr. Yost, Dick, and several of the other skiers arrived, Barney was carefully removing Kara's skis and pulling them from the snow.

The teacher knelt beside the girl and checked her pulse.

"I'm glad you didn't move her," he said. "She may have broken bones."

From the nearby road came the ambulance siren. Soon a rescue team came running with a specially outfitted toboggan onto which they moved Kara.

Barney, so worried about his friend he scarcely felt his own aches, put on his skis and followed Kara and the rescue crew to the road.

How still she was! Mr. Yost had assured him her pulse was quite strong. But why didn't she wake up?

As soon as she was in the ambulance, Barney started to ski away, but the teacher stopped him.

"You get in, too."

"I'm all right," insisted Barney.

"I want the doctor to go over you." Mr. Yost looked up at the cliff and shook his head. "I don't know how you're both alive."

Dick was standing beside the ambulance, shivering.

The teacher put his hand on the boy's shoulder. "Why don't you go along with your friends, Dick? I think it would be a help. You and Barney can ride in front with the driver. I'll take care of the skis and see you at the hospital. Oh, I'll phone your parents and Kara's."

The driver was not yet in his seat when Barney and Dick climbed in. The door shut behind them and they were alone.

"Was it Rokell?" demanded Dick.

"It must've been." That was all Barney had time to say before the driver leaped in.

At the hospital Kara was wheeled away, and then Barney was called for examination.

"I can't find anything wrong with you, except for a few bruises," said the doctor who looked him over. "I know that cliff. You must be a wonderful skier to come over that and live to tell about it."

"We rode the snowslide down," explained Barney. He had decided not to mention Rokell. "*Uh*—could we wait and find out how Kara is?"

"Oh, the girl. Sure. Have a seat. We'll let you know what we find."

Barney and Dick located chairs in a corner. Dick looked around as if making sure no one else was within earshot. Then he leaned close to Barney.

"Did you wonder why I didn't come after you when you and Kara went toward the cliff?" he asked.

Barney was surprised. "Of course not. That would've been stupid for you to follow us."

"Stupid or not, I was going to do it," he said. "But then I looked up the hill and saw the snow beginning to slide and I knew I'd better run for help."

"Good thing you did," said Barney. "That way you got the ambulance there in a hurry. If you'd come after us, there would've been three over the cliff. Rokell used some weird kind of power. We couldn't break away.''

"There's one thing that doesn't make sense,'' said Dick. "Why did he go to all that trouble and then go off without you?''

Barney had puzzled about that, too. "It could be he saw you and all the others coming and decided he had too big an audience.''

"Yeah.'' Dick ran his fingers through his wind-whipped hair, making it look wilder than before. "But why'd he drag Kara over the cliff?''

At the mention of Kara's name, Barney drew back. He couldn't think of her without pain.

Dick said, "Sorry. Guess you'd rather not talk about her.''

"Yes—well. I can't help thinking. Talking might help.'' He spoke more softly as a woman sat down a few chairs away. "I don't believe Rokell meant to take Kara over the cliff. I think he made a mistake and caught her in the same magnetic beam, or whatever, he aimed at me.'' Barney sighed deeply. "I blame myself.''

"Don't do that,'' said Dick. "You couldn't help it.''

"Thanks. Anyway, I'm glad you and the others got there fast. I'm sure that's why Rokell gave up.'' Barney leaned back in his chair and stared bleakly at the nurses' desk. "All we can do is guess. Who knows how that Gark thinks? Why'd he cover Kara up with snow?

106

Was that another one of his accidents?''

"Or was it so she couldn't see him pick you up?'' suggested Dick.

The door opened and Mr. Yost and Kara's parents joined the two boys. Fifteen minutes later a doctor came out and motioned them into an office.

He quickly reassured the MacDougalls, who sat down close together, their faces pale.

"We x-rayed your daughter,'' he said, "and didn't find any broken bones. She's still unconscious, but her pulse and breathing are good.''

Mrs. MacDougall asked anxiously, "But why is she still unconscious?''

"We don't know yet,'' the doctor answered. "We've put her to bed and will keep on checking her. You can go in and see her now. I'll take you up to her room.'' He turned to Dick, Barney, and Mr. Yost. "I know you're all concerned about the girl, but I'd rather have just the parents visit her right now.'' He seemed to read Barney's worried face, for he added, "Her chances are good. She's young and healthy.''

Young and healthy—and unconscious, thought Barney. All the way home in Mr. Yost's car, the word went over and over in his brain like a drumbeat—unconscious, unconscious. When would she come to? Would she ever wake up?

The teacher went into the house with Barney and,

107

after telling the Crandalls what had happened, he said, "You can be proud of your son. He kept his head all through this, and had already dug Kara out of the snow before we got there. If she pulls through, it's because of him."

His mother said gravely, "He can be depended on."

But weighed down by guilt, Barney took little comfort from the words of praise. If Kara hadn't stayed to help him when his bootlace broke, she'd be home now instead of in the hospital. That Rokell would stop at nothing to capture him, even if it meant harming someone else.

He longed to talk over his problem with his parents, but he knew from experience that he couldn't make them believe he was being pursued by a Gark from another planet.

Lost in his own thoughts, he forgot to feed Finn McCool until his mother reminded him. During dinner he found it impossible to follow the conversation. His father noticed his silence and remarked, "No wonder you're tired, after everything that happened today. And I know you're worried about Kara."

Exhausted, Barney fell asleep at once that night, but at six in the morning he was awake, staring into the predawn darkness, wondering how Kara was and trying to figure out what to do about Rokell.

He knew he couldn't count on Tibbo to help. He

hadn't heard from him since Tuesday night and today was Friday. While he turned restlessly in bed, the cold dawn light gradually brightened the room.

If it were only his own life that was in danger, it wouldn't be so bad. But look what had happened to Kara! He didn't know yet how badly she'd been hurt. And who would it be next time?

The only way he had even a chance of escaping Rokell was to stay near people. But if he did, it meant risking their lives.

When at last he made up his mind, he was satisfied that he had the right answer. But he dreaded what he had to do.

16 Ø

Captured!

Barney dozed, and when he woke again his first thought was of Kara. He wanted to call her parents, but he was afraid to do that. They must've been up late the night before. He'd feel like a rat if he awakened them.

As he limped toward the bathroom, he realized how stiff he was. No wonder, after dropping off that cliff.

In the healing comfort of a hot shower, he went over the plan he had made earlier in the morning.

All this time he had been trying to escape Rokell. Just as Tibbo had told him to do, he had stayed with people. Now he was going to stop using his family and friends as shields. He was going out alone to meet Rokell.

When he came out of the shower, his mother called up to him. "Mr. MacDougall just phoned. Kara's better. She's conscious, and the doctor says she's going to be all right."

Barney felt pounds lighter. But not even this welcome news could make him change his plan. The next time

Rokell came, his friends might not be so lucky. Barney knew he couldn't wait. The Gark might even be desperate enough to come to the house after him.

While he ate breakfast with his family, he had to keep reminding himself to act natural. Yet he couldn't keep from thinking that it might be the last time he'd sit at this table. His eyes went from one face to another and then back to his plate. He didn't want to show his emotion.

After he had helped clear the table, he went slowly upstairs to his room with Finn at his heels. Sitting on the bed, hugging his dog, he fought for control.

"I'll be back," he whispered.

Finn whined and licked his chin.

All the while Barney made his bed and straightened his room, Finn stayed close by, following him wherever he went.

Barney began talking to him as if he were a person. "I could write a letter to Dad and Mom," he said. "I could say I'm going out to meet Rokell face to face, but what good would it do? They wouldn't understand."

He felt safe talking out loud. His father had left for work and his mother and Scott were downstairs. All the time Barney talked, he continued to work. In a few minutes the bedroom was so neat it didn't look familiar.

Barney dropped onto the edge of his bed and Finn leaped up beside him. The soft fur and warm body were

111

comforting. Taking the dog's head between his hands, Barney looked into the round, dark eyes.

"If I don't come back," he said, "Dick will know Rokell got me and he'll tell Mom and Dad. So will Kara."

He gave his dog a last hug and got to his feet. "Don't you forget me," he said fiercely.

Finn stood on the bed with his head cocked to one side, watching curiously while his master started to the door, then came back to pick up his two hockey pucks.

"Scott always wants to play with these pucks," said Barney, as if it were important that the dog understand. "I never let him have them. I thought he'd lose them."

At this, Finn jumped down from the bed and trailed him into Scott's room where Barney stacked the pucks one on top of the other on the bookcase next to a stuffed monkey.

When he was ready to go outdoors, Barney located his mother at her desk in the living room, writing checks. Putting both hands on her slim shoulders, he said, "I'm going skiing for a while."

He leaned over and kissed her cheek.

With her eyes still on her work, she asked, "Is anyone going with you?"

"No." That was all he dared say because he couldn't trust his voice. He was glad his mother was too occupied with the bills to look up.

"I'm surprised you feel like skiing after that fall you had yesterday. Don't go far," she said. "It isn't safe to ski alone."

"I know." His hands tightened on her shoulders, and then he rushed out.

From the family room came the sound of a children's program on TV, but Barney didn't go in. He couldn't say good-bye to Scott. He knew if he talked to his brother he'd come apart for sure.

Finn McCool ran after him and stood with his nose to the back door, ready to go out.

"No way," said Barney firmly. "It might not be healthy for you around Rokell." With a final pat on Finn's head, he slipped out alone.

Outside, he quickly fastened on his skis and shoved off. He couldn't risk giving himself time to think.

His mother was right. He didn't feel much like skiing. The shower had not taken away all of the aches. But the meadow behind the house was the best place to be alone and attract Rokell's attention. The snow there was too deep for walking.

In the lee of the buildings the air was quiet but, as soon as he passed the garage, a wind whipped at him. Gusts raced across the open slope, raising a froth of snow.

Bearing right, he skied toward the foundation of the old barn, remembering the night last summer when

Tibbo had demonstrated his scientific power. He'd never forget how the shingles had sailed from the roof. Dick had said a magnetic force had pulled out all the nails.

The Garks had control of forces people on Earth didn't even know about. And Rokell was a Gark. In a contest Barney knew he wouldn't stand a chance. He only hoped he could reason with him and persuade him he was making a mistake.

So far Barney was skiing along in the usual way. No outside force pulled at him. Rokell might be waiting to be sure he was completely alone. Except for the cloud, there was no way of knowing when the outlaw Gark was about to attack because, even when he was near, Barney never felt the prickle of his skin that came when Tibbo contacted him.

When he came to the site of the old barn, he sat down sideways on the snow-covered stone wall, with his skis parallel to it. Looking up at the sky, he discovered a puffy cloud directly overhead. Rokell's cloud!

How should he talk with the hidden Gark?

Barney decided to take it for granted that Rokell was listening and that he could understand English as Tibbo did.

He spoke out loud. "Rokell, I'm here alone because I don't want anyone else to get hurt in case you're coming to get me."

The cloud above his head did not move, but another

cloud farther west began to float in Barney's direction.

What's this? he wondered. Had some Gark joined forces with Rokell?

Barney began talking again. "I'm not going to make trouble for you or any other Gark. But the way you act, you may draw attention to yourself. If I disappear, that will make people ask questions."

A shadow fell over Barney and the foundation of the old barn. A cloud—he wasn't sure which one it was— dropped lower and lower until the sky was blotted out.

Suddenly the cloud above him lifted slightly and began to foam and tumble like sea waves in a storm. Frightened by the strong winds that battered him, Barney crouched over his skis and covered his head with his arms.

Never in his life had he been so afraid, but he stood his ground.

In less than a minute the disturbance was over and there was silence except for a low, humming sound.

Barney stood up, shivering with cold and excitement. A cloud still shut out the sun.

"Barney!"

The shout came from the north, in the direction of the road. He turned his head quickly, and through white cloud-feathers saw Dick skiing toward him as fast as he could travel.

"Go back!" shouted Barney, motioning him away.

"Move! Move!" He tried to ski toward Dick to urge him to leave, but he couldn't make his feet go. Rokell must have him in his power.

The humming sound was louder. Barney looked up and saw in the center of the cloud above him a huge dark ball, slowly spinning.

"Rokell!" shouted Barney, shaking with fear. "Can you hear me?"

There was no answer, but he went on talking in the hope that the Gark was listening.

"All right, get me! But leave Dick alone!"

Dick called, "Hang in there! I'm coming!"

The cloud dropped around Barney, surrounding him with whiteness like a heavy snowstorm. Even when the spinning ball settled behind the foundation of the barn, he could barely see it.

Dick's voice reached him, this time near at hand. "Where are you? Say something so I can find you."

"Don't come any closer! Run!" cried Barney.

Dick's tall, thin figure appeared only an arm's length distant. "You're wasting your breath," he said stubbornly.

Barney couldn't help reaching out to him, even while begging him to go. "Hey, it's great to see you." His voice shook. "You know that. But, look, if you leave, maybe you can get help for me. Like you did when Kara

116

and I went over the cliff." That seemed like an argument that might appeal to Dick.

But Dick did not move. "Yeah? If I go, you'll disappear as soon as my back is turned. I'm staying." He stared past Barney. "What's that?"

Barney glanced over his shoulder. "Rokell's spaceship, I guess. He hasn't said anything, but he has me nailed to this spot."

"What?" said Dick. "You can get away. Try."

Barney made an effort to lift one of his skis. Nothing happened. "I can move my head and arms, but not my feet. You try."

"Sure," Dick said confidently. "No problem." A strange expression came over his face. "I'm stuck!"

"You wouldn't listen to me!" Barney said angrily. "I told you to stay away, and now it's too late! I came out here alone on purpose so no one else would get hurt, and now you've blown it!"

"You're right." Dick had turned pale. "I brought this on myself. I couldn't believe it was for real. Even after what happened to you and Kara yesterday, I guess I still thought it was an accident."

He waved his arms like a windmill and twisted from the waist, but his skis seemed to be rooted in the snow.

The humming sound that had been coming from the spaceship stopped.

"We're moving!" exclaimed Dick.

It was true. Like two robots they were sliding toward the ship.

Barney spoke through stiff lips. "Ornam, here we come."

Now they were close enough to see a door open in the side of the ball. A ramp slid down from it.

Helpless, the two boys were drawn smoothly up the ramp and through the doorway into darkness.

17 Ø

Space Flight

The door closed behind Barney and Dick, and the darkness gave way to a glow, revealing a small, bare chamber. Under their feet was a level floor, but the outer walls and ceiling were part of the curving ball.

Barney felt numb. The terrible wait was over. Rokell had him. The worst of it was, Dick was caught, too.

A voice spoke, though no one was in sight.

"Take off your skis and jackets. In this room you will be cleansed of all Earth germs and made immune to Gark germs."

"A decontamination chamber," muttered Dick. "I'm not taking anything off."

"Stop wasting time," the voice said briskly. "You can't walk around in a spaceship with skis on, and you'll be too warm in those coats."

"I've decided not to go," said Dick.

"Too late. You don't have a choice."

Barney bent to unfasten his skis. "You can't fight a Gark. We might as well do what he says."

Dick grumbled, "Oh, all right."

Barney found he was able to lift his foot from the ski, but as soon as he set it on the floor, he couldn't move it.

Dick was having the same problem. He met Barney's eyes. "We don't have a chance."

With a sick feeling, Barney watched the skis and jackets slide away and disappear into an opening in the floor which then closed.

Dick was right. Their chances of escaping from this powerful creature from space were zero. He could take them so far away they'd never see Earth again.

Boy, am I stupid! Barney scolded himself. I actually thought I could bargain with Rokell.

A hissing sound startled him out of his dark thoughts. Jets of air—or something that felt like air—ruffled his hair and Dick's. Clear, bright lights shone on them from ceiling, walls, and floor.

In a few seconds the hissing stopped and the light dimmed down to the soft glow. The wall in front of them lifted and fitted itself neatly against the ceiling. Straight ahead, in the center of the floor, were two seats that looked like molded plastic. They seemed to be fastened down like a dentist's chair.

Dick stepped forward. "Hey. I can walk!" He whirled around. "Where's the exit?"

Both boys ran to the spot where the door should have been but found only a smooth, curving wall that was as transparent as glass.

"Prepare for flight," said the voice. Under their feet came the humming sound they had heard before.

"We're going to blast off!" cried Dick excitedly.

The quiet voice filled the room. "Get into the chairs."

As soon as they were seated, the sides of the chairs folded over them, leaving only their heads and arms free. It was like being in a cocoon, thought Barney. At least Rokell was taking good care of them, and this was surprising. Come to think of it, the voice they had heard was pleasanter then he had expected Rokell's to be. If it belonged to the same creature who had taken Kara and him over the cliff, then Rokell must be two-sided like Dr. Jekyll and Mr. Hyde.

The humming noise speeded up until it was the buzz of an angry bumblebee. At the same time Barney felt as if he were in a rising elevator.

The cloud that had hidden the spaceship was becoming less dense and, through the clear walls of the slowly turning ball, he could see his home rapidly becoming smaller. They were on their way! A lump rose in his throat, making it hard to swallow.

But leaving no longer seemed to bother Dick. Now that they were airborne, his friend's fears appeared to

have been replaced by his scientific curiosity. The cocoons had opened and he was sitting upright, his head pivoting from side to side as he took in every possible view.

"How do they do it?" he marveled. "We're zooming up like a rocket, and I don't feel any big pull."

"We've learned to use electro-magnetic forces to simulate gravity in our spaceships," said the voice. "You'll feel the same as you do on Earth all the way to the moon."

"To the moon!" cried Barney. "I thought we were going to Ornam. Why are you taking us to the moon, Rokell?" Then, uncertainly, "Are you Rokell?"

"I am not," came the voice. "My name is Naf. I'm a friend of Tibbo. He told me to get on the scene and save you from Rokell."

Barney was dizzy with relief. "So Tibbo did reach you. He told me he'd try. Where is he now?"

"Good question," said Naf. "Last I heard he was picked up by one of our moonships somewhere between here and Jupiter."

"Where are you?" asked Dick.

"I'm not in the spaceship, if that's what you mean. I'm operating it by remote control. Actually, I'm on the moon."

"Was this ship in that other cloud I saw when I was out in the meadow?" asked Barney.

"It was."

Naf sounded smug and sassy, like Tibbo. And by the way he talked, he must have learned English the same way Tibbo had, by listening to TV and radio on his long journey from Ornam.

Naf went on. "Rokell took off like a comet when he saw this ship. I didn't even have time to freeze him."

"*Freeze* him?" To Barney this sounded like terrible punishment, even for Rokell.

"You know," said Naf impatiently. "I'd put him to sleep and slow down his breathing and all his life processes. Something like hibernation. When he'd wake up, he'd be in Ornam. Wouldn't hurt him any, but it would make him easier to handle."

"But why take us to the moon?" asked Barney.

"Because on the moon there are plenty of Garks to protect you. We can't spare anyone to chase Rokell or to guard you two full time on Earth."

Dick cut in. "How come you Garks can't capture Rokell when you're so powerful?"

Naf chuckled. "How come it takes a strong country like yours so long to catch some of your criminals?"

"You have a point there," admitted Dick.

"Rokell's clever." Naf sounded nervous. "And he doesn't give up. I'm sure he'll attack again before you reach the moon."

Great! thought Barney. He and Dick were alone in

this see-through ball, and Rokell was lying in wait for them. If something happened to Naf, they'd be done for.

Dick didn't seem worried. He had left his chair and was on his hands and knees staring back at Earth.

"Wow! Take a look! It's like a satellite weather map!"

Barney's mind was still on Rokell. "I wish I knew how to steer this ship," he muttered.

"Good idea," spoke up Naf. "I set it on computer, but we have a manual system, too, and you happen to be in the pilot's seat. See that handle in front of the right arm of your chair?"

"Yes."

"That's something like an airplane control. Pull it back, and the ship rises. Push forward, and the ship goes down. At present we're aiming directly at the moon. Dick, you'd better get back in your chair in case this new pilot flips the ship."

While Dick followed Naf's suggestion, Barney studied the moon. Still far ahead, but becoming larger with every second, the gray-white ball shone with a cool light. How strange and mysterious it looked, floating there in the darkness.

"It's—spooky," he whispered.

Barney had been talking only to himself, but Naf had heard. "Hard to understand how it keeps spinning up there, isn't it?"

126

Barney nodded in silence.

"You notice a sliver of the moon, a crescent, is reflecting the sun," Naf said. "The rest of it isn't as bright. It's lighted by Earthshine."

"Oh, that's it," said Barney. "Thanks." *Earthshine.* The sound of the word pleased him. He looked back at Earth, brilliant in technicolor, unlike the ghostly moon.

Dick was in his chair, and the sides had closed around him. Barney's chair enfolded him, too.

"Okay, I'm turning off the computer," Naf warned. "You're running the ship."

Barney's hand tightened on the steering lever. It did not seem to him that he moved it at all, but the spaceship turned sharply upward. Then, as he tried to correct his course, it swung to the left.

"Drunk driver," complained Dick.

Barney panted, "I've lost the moon." Hands damp with perspiration, he wrestled with the lever until the moon again swung into view.

Dick grumbled good-naturedly, "You're making me airsick."

"That's enough for now, Barney," said Naf. "We'll go back on the computer."

"Good!" Dick left his chair and returned to his study of the Earth.

"Yes, you're safe, Dick. But we're not through with the lesson," said Naf.

He next turned Barney's attention to what appeared to be a golden arrow at floor level. As Barney looked more closely, he saw that it was a beam of light.

"That's for defense," the Gark explained. "See that small wheel in the left arm of your chair? That controls the arrow. Turn it until the arrow points to an enemy, then push the red button next to the wheel. You'll send him flying. The harder you push, the farther he'll go."

"I don't see any gun," said Barney.

"Of course not. The actual weapon is under the floor. The arrow is the direction finder."

All of Barney's mind was taken up by the new skills Naf was teaching him. He forgot that his home was now thousands of miles behind him. He even forgot the danger of attack by Rokell.

In a few minutes Barney knew how to activate the power that flew the ship and how to open the storage compartments under the floor.

"You're a fast learner," commented Naf. "You have brains you've never used."

Barney was hurt. "I use my brains. I get good marks in school. Most of the time."

"You can do better," insisted Naf. "Try, and you'll be surprised."

Dick spoke up from his place on the floor. "Hey, Barney, I've been watching the daylight travel across the U.S. California's still dark, but it won't be for long."

Barney joined his friend. They had climbed so far, Earth was like the globe in his classroom. Now the Western Hemisphere was facing them. On the right the Atlantic Ocean was blue in the sun, and on the left it was still night over the Pacific.

Dick asked, "Naf, was this spaceship specially outfitted for us?"

"No. It's my own private transportation. When I got Tibbo's call, I didn't have time to do anything but toss in a couple of moon suits for you and send it off." There was a brief silence, then Naf cried, "There he is! Back to your seats!"

Rokell!

Barney and Dick leaped into the chairs and again the sides wrapped around them.

The humming sound cut off abruptly and the ball dropped like a stone. Only the protective cocoons saved the boys from flying out of their seats and hitting the ceiling.

Naf's voice, angry and ragged, reached their ears. "Rokell, you fool! Do you want this ship to crash on Earth?"

With a sickening lurch, the ball stopped its plunge. Again there was a humming under their feet and they began to rise.

"Look there!" Dick pointed upward toward a blimp-shaped object between them and the moon. "Must be Rokell."

As the long, oval ship came closer, a beam of light snaked toward them like a streak of lightning, missing them by inches.

"Quick!" ordered Naf. "Barney, get him!"

The order came too quickly for Barney. He had thought Naf was in control.

The arrow! In a panic he tried to remember how to aim it. He reached for the small wheel in the arm of the chair but, before he could touch it, the arrow swung around. Naf was again in charge, and the golden arrow pointed at the center of the oncoming ship.

18 Ø

Crash Landing

There was a sound like the pop of a pistol with a silencer on it. The space ball bucked. Most amazing of all, the blimp-shaped ship disappeared without a trace.

Barney stared in all directions, but Rokell's ship had vanished.

"Where'd he go?"

"I really blasted him." Naf sounded pleased with himself.

"Did you kill him?" asked Barney.

"Of course not. We don't kill. Life is the most precious thing in the universe."

"But that was a gun, wasn't it? What does it do if it doesn't kill?"

"I guess you could call it a gun," Naf conceded. "Call it a thruster gun. It thrusts the enemy away. It gave Rokell a fast ride. I'm sure we'll beat him to the moon now. No thanks to you, Barney."

Barney reddened. "I couldn't think what to do."

"I don't blame you, Earth boy," said Naf. "For a second or two Rokell cut off my power, so I hoped you could take over. Of course, you can't react as quickly as a Gark."

Earth boy! What was wrong with being an Earth boy? Barney's eyes shone with anger. "Earth people are just as good as Garks! How'd I know you were going to turn the ship over to me?"

"Wow! I started a fire!" Naf sounded amused. "Let's forget Rokell. We're getting close to the moon."

Still hurt and indignant, Barney gazed down at the moon's pale surface. It was close enough so he could see the round craters and the rough piles of rock.

How lonely it was!

"It's like a desert," remarked Dick.

Barney added, "It's like the pictures the astronauts took."

"What'd you expect?" asked Dick with a smile.

Naf spoke. "Say good-bye to Earth. We're going to circle behind the moon. That's where our base is."

Earth, a blue, white, and brown ball floating in blackness, now appeared to be smaller than the moon.

"Put on your moon suits," said Naf. "You'll need them as soon as we land. On this ship you've had good air to breathe, but on the moon you'll have to carry your own oxygen."

Moon suits. Barney was ready to ask, "Where are

132

they?'' But then he knew. Feeling proud at remembering, he pushed the brown button in the arm of his chair. At once a door opened in the floor and there were the suits.

Barney lifted them out of the storage compartment and handed one to Dick, who held it up critically. ''It'll never fit me. It's too small.''

''Don't be so sure,'' said Naf. ''They stretch.''

Naf proved to be right. The suits were comfortable to wear and, inside the bubble that covered their heads, it was easy to breathe. The clear helmet, similar to a fishbowl, clamped onto a firm rim at the neck of the suit.

Dick walked around, trying out the new costume. ''This is neat.'' His voice had a different tone than usual.

''You sound like a radio,'' said Barney.

Dick answered, ''So do you.''

''You each have your own electronic system,'' Naf said. ''Since there's so little air on the moon, your ordinary voice wouldn't carry.''

Dick reached over his shoulder to touch the little tank fastened high on his back. ''How does this work?'' he asked, curious as always. ''I didn't switch on any oxygen, but I know I'm breathing it.''

''It works automatically as soon as you put on the helmet,'' Naf explained. ''By the way, we've reached the far side of the moon. This is the side you never see from Earth.''

The land below was a jumble of mountains. In the glaring sunlight, the ground changed from grayish white to sandy brown and back to white again. Mountains cast ink-black shadows.

Dick said doubtfully, ''I can see we're going to breathe all right, but how are these thin suits going to keep us from roasting in the hot sun? Or freezing when it's dark? I've read the temperature goes up to boiling and down a long way below zero.''

''Don't worry,'' said Naf. ''Those suits have temperature controls. Look what's just ahead. We're approaching Gark Base.''

Barney caught a glimpse of several spaceships on the ground. Some were small and round like the one in which he and Dick were riding. Others were more like Rokell's long ship. Judging by the sizes, Barney reasoned that the larger ones were intergalactic spaceships, used for travel from one galaxy to another. The smaller ones were probably like taxis, for short trips.

Next he caught sight of a movement. Looking more closely, he was bewildered at what he saw. What appeared to be a huge brown caterpillar glided from a hole in the side of a mountain and continued at a steady pace across the uneven ground to a crater, where it went over the edge and vanished.

"What's that?" Barney pointed. "That—that long thing that came out of the hole."

Naf howled with laughter. "That's soil and rocks we're clearing out of the middle of the mountain. Our base will be in that cave. Safer that way. We'll be protected from falling meteorites."

Barney was about to ask where the workers were when Naf's excited cry made him forget the view below.

"Quick! Into your seats! Rokell's back! I'm losing control of the ship. Take over, Barney!"

But again Barney didn't have a chance. Before he could reach the safety of the chair, the ship rose upward like a kicked football and sailed past the Gark base.

The boys slid from one side of the ball to the other until Barney managed to grab the pedestal of his chair. Dick caught hold of his friend's foot and clung to it. Even then, the ride was so rough they couldn't climb into the chairs.

Fifteen minutes later, the ship jolted to the moon surface, the door rolled open, and the boys tumbled down the ramp onto the powdery dust of the moon.

Barney sat up and looked around, trying to get his

bearings. Not far off, Rokell's spaceship was settling down as lightly as a bird.

At once Barney knew there was no use running away. In the open, on this rough, barren surface, they'd be caught easily. Naf's spaceship was the only protection they had.

Dick was sitting at the foot of the ramp, head bent forward and shoulders slumped.

"Come on!" urged Barney. "Let's get back in the ship."

Dick did not move. Frightened, Barney took hold of his shoulder. At the touch, his friend fell sideways onto the ground.

Barney was terror stricken. What had happened to Dick?

Seizing the unconscious boy under the arms, he pulled him up the ramp into the spaceship, then rushed to the controls on the chair arm.

For one desperate moment he couldn't remember which button closed the door. He concentrated as never before in his life.

The blue one!

To his relief, the door shut as soon as he touched the button.

After racing back to Dick, Barney dropped to his knees and studied the pale face inside the bubble. Dick's eyes were closed but his mouth was open as if he were gasping. Gasping for air!

Removing Dick's helmet would be too much of a risk, Barney realized. After the crash landing and the opening of the door, the air in the spaceship might be as poor as moon air. They would have to depend on their own supply.

Barney rolled Dick onto his side to check the tube that connected the oxygen tank to the head covering. The tube seemed okay, but he felt a stir of air at the stiff neckband where helmet and suit joined. A second later he discovered the problem. A clamp was unfastened. Oxygen was leaking out. As soon as Barney snapped the clamp shut, the air loss stopped.

In a short time Dick began to breathe more easily and his face was less pale. His chest rose and fell at an even rate.

There was nothing else Barney could do for his friend, but he stayed beside him, hoping to see his eyes open.

Still on his knees beside Dick, Barney cast a quick glance toward Rokell's ship, worried about what the Gark might be doing. One look held him fascinated, unable to tear his eyes away.

Something was pouring through the open doorway. At first it seemed like a horde of angry bees, especially

137

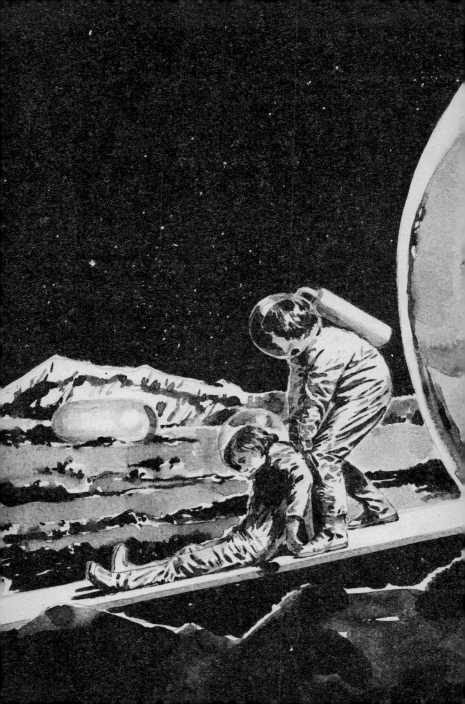

since he could hear a high-pitched humming sound. What *was* it?

Barney stood up and stared. Curiosity and fear warred in his brain.

The humming became a roar, and a cloud of small grayish objects shot upward. High above the surface, they spread out in a great shadow that darkened the moonscape. They reminded Barney of a movie he had seen about a plague of locusts that appeared every seven years, blotting out the sun, then settling to devour all the crops and every blade of grass.

If these things that had come out of Rokell's ship were locusts, they had come to the wrong place for dinner. They wouldn't find even a leaf on the moon.

A voice boomed from the dark cloud. "Barney, come out!"

Surprised and frightened, Barney shook like a loose-jointed puppet. At last he managed to answer, "What—what do you want?" His voice, magnified by the power inside his helmet, carried out of the spaceship and up to the cloud.

Rokell's reply came back, "I want you! You're the enemy of all Garks!"

"No, I'm not!" cried Barney. Then he asked fearfully, "Are you Rokell?"

"I am!" As Rokell spoke, the thousands of gray ob-

140

jects roared together into a column. The sun, no longer hidden, glinted on the flying particles.

Paralyzed by fear, Barney watched the moving column twist and turn above him as if it were alive.

He had to do something to save himself and Dick. With his eyes still turned upward, he backed away until he bumped into the pilot's chair. With a trembling hand, he pulled the steering lever back sharply.

The ship should have leaped upward, but nothing happened.

There was no humming sound, he realized. The power must have gone off at the time of the rough landing. In his panic Barney couldn't remember how to reactivate it. Just as before, his mind went blank. Naf was right. An Earth boy was no match for a Gark.

But was that true? An Earth boy with a Gark's machine might do all right. This idea seemed to clear Barney's brain. Sure of himself now, he put his forefinger on the yellow button. In response, power purred beneath his feet.

Great! Now the steering handle should work. It *had* to work!

He pulled back on the lever, expecting the ship to rise. Nothing happened. In desperation he yanked the stick in all directions, but the spaceship remained motionless. The rough landing had done more than switch off the power. Apparently it had damaged the flight controls.

That meant there was no hope. Whatever those small things were that were flying overhead, it had taken great energy to hurl them into the sky. That same force could easily destroy this small ship.

Looking up again through the clear top of the space ball, Barney saw that the gray objects had taken the form of a huge snake, coiled and ready to strike. As he watched, the snake began to dive.

19 Ø

The Red Button

Although there was no hiding place in the transparent spaceship, Barney raced across the floor and pulled Dick close to the pilot's chair to give him what protection he could.

He was crouched over his friend when the strange objects struck the spaceship like hailstones. In seconds they whirled on and were out of sight.

Barney looked around the ship in amazement. The entire outer surface of the ball was pockmarked from the brief attack, but the holes didn't seem to come through to the inside. He did notice in several places something sharp still embedded in the outside wall.

His first impulse was to run out and seize one of the particles but he held back, knowing it would be suicide to leave the ship. It was his only protection.

Soon he discovered one of the missiles was stuck in the clear wall at eye level. Moving closer, he could see it was about three inches long and shaped like a dagger.

143

Barney shuddered as he imagined what all those little daggers could do to a human body. And it was certain that Rokell would come back again and again until he broke through to his victims.

If only I could talk with Dick! thought Barney. Together they might come up with an idea, but his friend still lay unconscious.

A new noise, the sound of an approaching railroad train, reached Barney's ears. That was impossible. There were no trains on the moon! But when he looked in the direction of the sound, he saw something worse than a train. To his horror, what appeared to be a tornado was weaving its way toward him. That must be it. He had often heard that a tornado roared like a train coming near.

This must be Rokell, on his way back again. The gray daggers were whirling around a deadly center. This strange tornado could pick up the space ball and smash it to bits on the rocks.

Barney was frantic. He had to do *something*.

As his eyes darted around the inside of the ship in a vain search for help, his attention was suddenly caught. Most of the floor was flooded with sunlight, but the shadows cast by the two chairs in the center of the ball were inky black. In one of those dark patches the golden arrow shone like a beacon. The sight reminded him that the power was on. It was still humming under the floor.

The thought flashed into his mind. Was it possible

some of the controls worked, even though the flight lever wouldn't operate? He rushed to the chair and sat down.

His hand went to the little wheel in the left arm of the chair. He turned the wheel with his forefinger, and to his delight the golden arrow moved in response.

Deliberately he spun the wheel until the arrow on the floor pointed at Rokell's oncoming tornado. With his finger poised above the red button, Barney waited.

The roar of the tornado grew louder. Bits of flying dirt and rock thudded against the wall of the ship. The ship itself began to sway from the advancing whirlwind.

Barney didn't dare wait any longer. Checking to be sure the arrow was pointing at the whirlwind, his finger came down hard on the red button.

The gentle *pop* was the same sound he had heard when Naf fired at Rokell's spaceship.

At first it seemed nothing had happened. Then the ship gradually stopped wobbling. Through the clear sides of the ball, Barney could see the tornado, but it was moving more slowly. It was shrinking, becoming shorter and shorter. The roar became a mumble and finally—with a faint sound like a breath of wind or a sigh—the tornado vanished. Nothing was left of Rokell except the long spaceship in which he had arrived. Even the little daggers had disappeared, though the moon dust did seem to be darker than before.

What have I done? wondered Barney. Naf had said

pushing the red thruster button would send an enemy flying. But Rokell hadn't flown away. He had shrunk to nothing.

Staring through the clear walls of the spaceship, Barney noticed a motion outside. Dust was spinning around like a whirlpool, like a miniature tornado.

That was strange. There was no wind on the moon—except for Rokell. Rokell had seemed to be made of wind and daggers.

Barney peered more closely at the column of twirling dust outside the spaceship. In some weird way, was that Rokell?

A sound behind him made Barney whip around.

Dick was sitting upright on the floor, shaking his head inside the clear bubble of his helmet.

"What happened?" he asked. "Last I knew I was falling down the ramp."

"You passed out," said Barney. "One of the clamps on your helmet came unfastened and the oxygen was leaking. I fixed it. It's okay now."

"Oh, man! That could've been curtains. Thanks!" He began to stand up, but he tottered on his feet.

Barney took hold of his arm and helped him to one of the chairs where he lay back and closed his eyes.

"Where's Rokell?" he asked wearily.

"I—I'm not sure. I shot him with the thruster gun."

Dick sat up and opened his eyes. "What!"

"I had to," said Barney. "He attacked the ship once and he was on his way back with a tornado."

Dick was staring at him in disbelief.

"You should've seen him!" Barney cried, thinking to himself that he was always in trouble because he saw things no one else did. "He was a lot of little daggers—thousands of them. Look what they did to the spaceship." He pointed to the marks on the hard shell of the ball. "Some of the daggers are stuck there, too."

Dick glanced upward. "Yeah, I see a few little sharp things. But where are the rest of them? You said thousands."

Barney looked outside. Only rocks and dirt met his gaze. "I—I'm not sure."

"Did you blast them across the moon?" suggested Dick.

"No, they just . . ." Barney, feeling a familiar prickle, stopped trying to explain. He held up his hand for silence. "Tibbo," he whispered.

The prickles were strong. Tibbo must be nearby.

20 Ø

Reunion on the Moon

A round shadow drifted across the barren surface of the moon.

Barney pressed the blue button and was glad to see that it, too, was in working order. The door slid open and he ran outside just in time to see Tibbo's mini ship come to the ground.

Waving excitedly, he walked as best he could in the low gravity toward the ball with the ring around the middle. The door of the newly arrived spaceship opened and the feeling of prickles grew even stronger.

Barney came to a halt and stared, watching for the first glimpse of his space friend.

At first he could see nothing. Then he noticed a sparkle like sunlight on an ice-coated bush. Or like hundreds of gold needles floating in the air. It was a welcome change from the menace of Rokell's daggers.

"Barney!"

It was Tibbo's voice, cheerful, warm. The cluster of

shining needles came closer and closer until Barney was surrounded by prickles. It was like being hugged by a friendly porcupine.

He held out his arms, trying to touch his space friend. "Tibbo! Don't you have a body?"

"Of course I do! But I'm not using it. It gets in the way, especially on the moon. I'd have to wear a special suit like you. My body's back in an air chamber at the Gark base."

"But—but what *are* you?" stammered Barney.

"I guess you could say right now I'm pure energy. These shining needles, as I read you calling them, are the thinking power of my brain and the strength of my body. It's wonderful! I feel so free!" The shimmering needles leaped into the air and drifted down again as light as dandelion seeds.

"But Rokell. He wasn't little needles like you. He was a—tornado of daggers."

"Oh, Rokell." The glowing prickles bounced in front of Barney and stopped. "Energy can take different shapes. I'm a bunch of electro-magnetic needles. Rokell turned his power into daggers and wind because he wanted to scare you."

"He did that, all right. I thought we were done for," said Barney.

"Rokell didn't have killing in mind," argued Tibbo. "What he wanted was to take you back to Ornam alive.

He must've thought you'd give yourself up when you saw his tornado.''

Barney felt doubtful. "You can think what you want to. I don't trust that Gark."

"You gave him a surprise, that's for sure." Tibbo began to chuckle. "Imagine. An Earth boy defeated a Gark. That's a record. I'm proud of you, Barney."

"Thanks. And thanks for sending Naf to rescue us. What happened to him?"

"He's still at the Gark base. When I flew in there a few minutes ago he was going wild trying to get in touch with you. He told me you and Rokell headed this way, so I parked my body, switched to the mini ship, and came looking for you."

Barney's worries returned. "Did I kill Rokell?"

"No. The thruster gun acts differently on pure energy than on a solid spaceship. The shot turned the daggers into dust and broke up Rokell's tornado. It was like letting the air out of a balloon."

"Yeah. He's an awfully small wind now." Barney pointed to the column of whirling dust no more than two feet high.

"That's Rokell, all right," said Tibbo. "Wait while I send him on his way."

Dick had been sitting on the ramp outside the spaceship, listening to the conversation. Now, looking rested, he came over and joined Barney.

He said smugly, "I could hear what Tibbo said."

"Look! There he goes," said Barney.

Tibbo sped off, becoming long and narrow like a flying dragon, chasing the little whirl of dust across the moonscape and into the long spaceship. As soon as the door closed behind what was left of Rokell's energy, the ship rose upward.

The golden needles came toward the boys.

"Hi, Dick," said Tibbo. "I've sent Rokell back to the Gark base. They'll recharge his energy there, then ship him, body and all, to Ornam for reprograming. He'll never bother you again."

"Good!" said Barney. He wondered how two creatures from the same planet could be as different as Rokell and Tibbo. But of course there were all kinds of people on Earth, too.

"What do you mean, reprograming?" asked Dick.

"I mean he'll be taught to stop thinking everyone who isn't a Gark is an enemy. He's worth saving. He'll have five hundred more years of useful life."

"I'm glad I didn't kill him!" Barney didn't want to kill any creature, even Rokell. Taking a leap for joy, he shot high off the ground and would have fallen when he came down if Dick hadn't caught him.

"Easy," warned Tibbo. "The moon has only one-sixth the gravity of Earth, so you don't weigh much here."

151

"How come I can talk with you?" asked Dick. "Barney says I never could hear you before."

"Special moon privilege," said Tibbo.

"Thanks," said Dick. "It's great to be able to hear you. And—a request. I've forgotten everything that happened when you were on Earth last summer. Can you make me remember?"

"Of course. Hold still."

Dick stood without moving, his long legs far apart and his feet planted firmly on the moon dust. Tibbo's golden needles clustered around his helmet, making him resemble a beekeeper surrounded by golden bees.

"I remember," said Dick slowly, as if he were in a trance. "I see a spaceship. It looks like the one you came in today. Barney's standing in front of it. He looks scared."

The cluster of needles flew away from Dick, single file. Tibbo's voice said, "It all will come back to you."

Dick shook himself. "Thank you! Thank you! Will I keep on remembering? And when I get back to Earth will I know I've been on the moon?"

"Yes to both questions," Tibbo answered.

"Hey, Barney! I remember!" shouted Dick. "And we're actually on the moon," he added, as if he had just fully realized where he was. He grabbed Barney's hands and the two friends jumped around in a circle, balancing each other and shouting, "The moon! We're on the moon!"

Tibbo leaped beside them like animated tinsel.

At last, tired of circling, the boys strolled around, looking for small rocks to take home.

In this low gravity, it seemed easiest to walk with knees slightly bent. When Barney wanted to stop to pick up something, he found he had to plan three steps ahead of time or he'd keep on going.

"Wouldn't Scott have fun here!" he said.

Dick laughed. "I'd like to see Finn McCool bouncing along."

"I wish Kara could've come." Barney stood still, letting his mind travel back to Earth. "Anyway, I have some moon rocks for her. And a couple for Scott."

"Okay, you two. It's time to leave," called Tibbo. "We'll go back in my ship. Naf's crate needs repairs."

Barney hopped toward Naf's space ball. "Have to get our skis and jackets."

In less than five minutes they were back in space, high above the rocks and craters of the moon.

Tibbo said, "You can take off your moon suits now. I'll have you home in half an hour, in time for lunch."

Barney looked toward the shining needles. Right now they were arranged in a diamond shape, perched on the floor on one point.

In a few minutes he'd be saying good-bye to Tibbo. Once he had thought he didn't want him to come back. But now the boy from Ornam had become part of his life. He couldn't bear to lose touch with him.

"Will you come to see us again?" he asked.

"You can be sure of it. We Garks have plans for getting in touch with Earth leaders after we're studied your solar system. That'll be in ten or fifteen years."

"We'll be grown up by then," said Barney. "But I doubt if we're Earth leaders that soon."

"You two can play an important part, all the same, so prepare for it. You can help humans and Garks understand each other."

Dick's eyes shone. "Swell. We'll be looking for you."

"Good." Tibbo's voice went on. "If the rest of Earth people are like you boys, we can work together and have millions of years of peace and progress."

It sounded great, thought Barney. He wondered how he could get ready. First he wanted to learn more about space—the universe. Now he could understand why Dick was so interested in science.

"Don't wait ten or fifteen years before you come back," urged Barney. "I want to know how you like Mars and Venus. It'd be great to have you for a neighbor."

Tibbo answered with a smile in his voice. "I hope the rest of your world feels like that. Humans and Garks could do a lot for each other."

The cluster of needles moved in front of something that looked like a TV set. The screen lighted and a picture came into focus.

154

Barney leaned closer. "That's my house. That's where I live."

"Right," said Tibbo. "You're looking at my Earth scanner. There's your mother coming out the back door with your little brother and Finn McCool."

Barney drew in a deep breath. "She'll never believe I've been on the moon."

"She'll believe you," said Tibbo. "We'll land in the back yard." He turned off the scanner.

The Earth came closer—blue and white and beautiful.

Home, thought Barney. The whole doggone Earth was home.

ABOUT THE AUTHOR

The backgrounds of MARGARET GOFF CLARK's books range from the Niagara frontier where she and her husband, Charles, live, to the Muskoka region of Ontario, Canada, to Texas, and now to the moon.

"I like to be at home in the places my characters inhabit," says Mrs. Clark. "This has led to working vacations on a lobstering island off the coast of Maine for *Mystery of Sebastian Island* and on the Gulf Coast of Texas for *Who Stole Kathy Young?* But for *Barney in Space* I've had to rely on scientific sources, especially the accounts of the astronauts."

Such favorite activities as swimming, hiking, canoeing, and mountain climbing (small mountains) have further contributed ideas and background for her eighteen books.

Margaret Clark believes her experience as a schoolteacher and mother influenced her to write for young readers. That, and her own pleasure in reading and writing "stories that move."

ABOUT THE ARTIST

TED LEWIN has illustrated many books for children, and is the author of three *World Within a World* books—*Everglades, Baja,* and *Pribilofs*. He lives in a restored brownstone in Brooklyn with his wife, Betsy, who is also an artist and author.